HELL BORN

THE GUILD OF SHADOWS 1

MARIE BILODEAU

This book is a work of fiction. Any resemblance to persons, living or dead, or places, events or locations is purely coincidental.

Cover art by Éric Belisle.

Cover design by Ânia Loureiro.

Editing by Jessica Torrance.

❀ Created with Vellum

*To Brandon Crilly, without whom Tira wouldn't exist and
the world would be a more boring place*

ACKNOWLEDGMENTS

End of 2017, fellow writer Brandon Crilly contacted me to ask if I would like to join a Dungeons & Dragons campaign. "I'm not sure," said I, "I'm busy." "Here are the people who have agreed to play," said he. "Oh," said I.

So I agreed, but insisted I didn't have the time to build a character. I believe I heard his eyes roll over text, but he obliged and, a week later, handed me the sheet for a courser – a bounty hunter rogue – with instructions to come up with a name and personality.

"I'll call her Tira Misu, because dessert and stabbing, ha ha ha ha ha!" was my answer.

More eye rolling and obliging.

I came up with a basic character based on that. She had a code, and that code made her fiercely loyal to her friends, while making her a bit stabby to people she perceived as bad. But she was willing to redefine that should her friends need her to.

Because she was built as reactive to her friends and their emotions and needs, Tira became fleshed out thanks to the people surrounding the table, and how they interacted with her. She became who she is thanks to my #writersintaldorei crew – Jay Odjick, Evan May, Derek Künsken, Tyler Goodier, Nicole Lavigne and Matt Moore.

A bunch of the characters in this novel are based on the characters skillfully played by them, though the story, world and everything else is very much not at all it.

We ended arc 1 of our campaign after almost two years. I wasn't ready to let go of these characters, both the ones who lived and the ones who perished along the journey. (You can read all about that at www.mariebilodeau.com/dd-taldorei/, should you be interested.)

This is my chance to play with them again, and give Tira an entirely new direction to grow into.

Aside from my game buddies, I also couldn't have finished this book without Kerri Elizabeth Gerow, who has supported me for the length of my career and still seems to love me. Same for my sister-in-law, Jessica Torrance, who was instrumental in forging this book, both as its transcriber and editor.

I could thank so many more people and always

have, but I'll close off by thanking two more: my mom, Suzanne Desjardins, for her artistic spirit and kindness.

And you, the reader, who followed me through various SF genres and still voraciously pick up my books. You inspire me to keep going, and I will always be grateful for that.

I COULDN'T SPOT Clay from where I crouched. The moon hid behind thick clouds, the stars followed suit, and we'd killed the two lamps lining this street. I could see fine in darkness, as could Clay.

But Clay wasn't messing around with sneakiness tonight. That put me on high alert, since Clay liked messing around with pretty much everything, as long as he thought he could get away with it.

Without that minor indication that I should take this seriously, I doubt I would. This place didn't exactly signal danger. The whole area smelled of incoming summer, some keener having even cut his yellow grass already. No insect buzzed about the darkness, nor did any dog bark, even though I suspected that at least every second house had a well-groomed, purse-sized puppy.

The street was as suburbia as suburbia could get. That didn't exactly bring me joy. My foster family had lived in suburbia. And that hadn't gone so great.

What the hell are we doing here?

I hadn't asked Clay before coming, because I never felt the need to ask. It's not like I had anything better going on tonight. And, depending on how tomorrow went, this might be our last outing for a while.

Maybe forever.

Movement across the yard caught my attention and I focused on it, my eyes able to pierce the shadows of this world as easily as they would be able to see in daylight. Probably more easily, in fact. The shadows brought comfort that daylight just couldn't.

From the quick, effortless movement, I was certain it was Clay. He headed toward a two-story, simple-looking family home, just different enough from its nearby neighbor to be called unique. As long as you didn't look down the street at all the "slightly different unique" homes, anyway. They were all squished against one another, too, like they lived under eternal roll call.

Kinda like Clay and I did, except when we managed to sneak out for a spell or two.

My job tonight was pretty simple. Keep an eye out for anyone coming home earlier than anticipated. Clay would slip into the home, disable the security system (stabbing often proved a functional means of doing that), grab whatever we'd been sent here to retrieve, and then get the hell out.

I wondered if Clay even needed me, and figured he just wanted a friend along for the ride. Or someone to watch his back, I suppose. Still, this was pretty boring.

My tail twitched behind me, and I forced it to remain still. Having a demon tail was bad enough, so I tried to keep it as still and unseen as possible.

I folded the shadows around me as I moved up the neighbor's driveway, to ensure I wouldn't be seen.

Folding the shadows is the best way I'd found to describe it, but it was really more like stepping into them. Becoming one of them. Vanishing from sight, or at least becoming the thing people spot out of the corner of their eye when they feel like they might not be alone.

Stories of demons hiding in the shadows might not have been true and just figments of terrified imaginations beforehand, but now? It was true.

All of it.

It became true when I was seven years old, terrified of my foster father who lived in a house just like this, and I'd folded the shadows around me to vanish.

It was the first time I'd felt safe.

I felt safe now, folded in those shadows, even though we were in suburbia, even though the street was as quiet as a midnight graveyard.

Clay vanished by the side of the targeted house. I

slipped around its other side, near some bud-riddled bushes, tiny leaves daring to pierce into the night. I grinned at them and debated breaking into the house, but decided to stick to the plan and keep an eye on anyone coming our way. The tiny leaves would be good enough company for a boring evening.

I didn't even know how the bush managed to survive. There were maybe six feet between this house and the next. Three windows were perfectly aligned on each house, and I imagined they were tall enough that you weren't in constant danger of seeing your neighbors naked.

I hoped so, anyway.

But the bush had made this its place, and somehow still thrived despite the snug quarters and lack of light.

"Good little bush," I whispered to it. I was debating pulling it out of the ground and finding a new spot for it when I heard a noise from the house Clay had snuck in. It wasn't loud, though loud enough to catch my ear, and I wasn't exactly near one of the tall windows. Maybe I'd misheard and it had come from the other house?

Thud.

This time I was sure it had come from the targeted house. And I knew Clay wasn't a klutz.

Shit. Someone had gotten in. Or had been waiting in there.

I decided to go in the window for maximum

surprise, but just as I was about to hoist myself up, the window shattered as someone jumped from one house directly into the next. I covered my head, shards of cheap glass showering down on me. No self-respecting demon girl went on a heist wearing anything that couldn't take cheap glass showers, so my purple skin was mostly unaffected. A dribble of blood streamed down my face, but that was it.

"I'll be back," I told the bush, pushed myself off the side of the building and onto the next, as quick as a hyper feline, and grabbed the edge of the window where the intruder had disappeared. Clay wasn't following, which worried me a bit, since he loved a good fight. I'd have to get to him later.

First, this maniac running around had to be stopped.

I heaved myself over the window ledge and crunched down on some pieces of glass, wincing. The shadows were still comfortably folded around me, but that wouldn't stop sound from travelling. Might as well put a big target sign right over me.

I shifted off the glass, wincing again at two more loud steps, and then my boots found quieter ground. A door slammed downstairs.

Damn it!

I leapt off the banister and cleared the stairs in one bound, crouching and then leaping at the door, throwing it open. I wrapped the shadows more deeply onto me as I threw myself off the stairs and to the right, in case anyone was waiting to fire a weapon.

But no one did. In fact, no one did anything. I'd expected some kind of chase, but when I looked up and down the dark street, no one moved.

I stood as quiet as the shadowfs, trying to spot someone or something. The air felt crisper, like winter debated whether or not it wanted to re-establish dominance. I felt bad for the bush.

Another scent caught my attention. Burn. Something was burning.

Orange flickering danced in the darkness of the house next door, the curtains covering its front bay windows going up in flames, the window cracking under the heat.

Clay!

I ran for the other house, opting to go through the window and avoid the fire licking the main door. I pulled myself up in a mirror image of the house I'd just been in, except this one was filling up with smoke, fast.

No self-respecting purple-skinned demon girl would also leave home without a face mask, so I pulled it up to cover my mouth and nose, my eyes watering at the smoke. I found the stairs and carefully went down them.

A large lump in the middle of the living room, near the fire, caught my eye. I headed to it and started tugging at Clay. Damn he was heavy. And who'd managed to knock him out? I'd never seen that happen, and I'd seen him take some spectacular blows!

I grunted and pulled at him, yanking him toward the back door as the fire caught hold of the wall below the stairs, drawn up by the broken window.

Clay grunted, his eyes blinking as I flipped him on his back without meaning to. He was just so damn hard to move! Why was he so heavy? Was I that tired?

The bay window up front cracked and shattered, the fire dancing more fiercely at the fresh intake of air.

Another good yank and I reached the back door. I wish I knew more about how fire travelled, but hoped the air upstairs and at the front of the house would stop the fire from channeling this way.

I opened the back door, smoke rushing our way, and ducked lower, coughing. I grabbed Clay by the armpits and pulled as hard as I could. The second we cleared the threshold, it felt like he lost about a hundred pounds, sending us both flying into the backyard.

He grunted and shifted, seemingly regaining consciousness. A quick glance didn't immediately reveal an injury. His dark eyes seemed to focus, his skin held no mark, his dark hair, well, that always looked a mess. His clothing seemed undisturbed…what the hell had happened?

A scream ripped from the top of the house. Chills gripped my spine.

Someone was in the house. And it sounded like a little girl.

"Get to safety," I told Clay, who worked at standing up. He coughed and gave me a thumbs up.

"Careful," he managed to choke out.

I grinned at him. "Always am." He grunted, which only made me grin more.

I ran to the side of the house, deciding to take the express to the second floor and ignore the probably fiery stairs. I jumped up the side of the other house, kicked toward the burning house and gripped the window ledge, pulling myself up, instinctively wrapping the shadows around me.

The orange hue of the fire flickered in the stairwell, and grew brighter by the second. I didn't have much time.

Sobbing to my left. Where the hell were the fire engines and their blaring horns? At least they didn't cover the child's soft sounds, I suppose.

I headed toward the sobs quickly, ignoring the crunching of glass under my feet.

A child's room. Very pink. Very cute. Very empty.

Where the heck was the kid? And the parents, for that matter?

Flames joined the light, the heat rising exponentially, the smoke so thick I had to crouch beneath it. Even then, my eyes stung. I wouldn't last long.

The fire raged loudly, blocking out the sobbing. Where would a kid…it dawned on me. The kid's closet was closed. Of course she'd be in there.

Closets held monsters until the rest of the house held monsters. Then, they were safe ground.

I opened the door. The little girl looked up from where she'd scrunched herself into a ball, holding a stuffed unicorn, which was predictably pink.

"Come on," I said as delicately as I could. The kid looked up with wonder and some panic.

Of course, she couldn't see me. I sighed. Seeing me wouldn't exactly make her feel safer.

"Close your eyes. I'm an angel come to get you to safety," I said, looking back at the incoming flames before focusing back on the girl. We had thirty seconds, tops.

The girl's eyes weren't closed, now wide with wonder. I sighed. "I'm an angel *unicorn*," I added for good measure. She seemed even more pleased. "But I can't touch you unless your eyes are closed. I can whisk you to safety if you close your eyes."

She debated for a few seconds, then closed her eyes. Finally. Damn kids and their need for reassurance.

I swooped her up in my arms. Now that she was in the folded shadows with me, she could see me easily. If she opened her eyes.

"Keep them closed, or we'll both fall," I said in my most dramatic, whimsical voice. Which probably still made me sound slightly demonic, but hey, points for effort.

She nodded and scrunched her face more. I grinned and opened the window. The fire filtered into the bedroom, and the floor felt much warmer than it should.

Second story wasn't bad. I had little respect for many things, including gravity. Well, gravity at this height. My respect for it grew the higher I got.

I jumped out into the backyard, landing hard on my feet, trying to absorb the blow for the little girl. I was pretty sure human kids were fairly breakable.

"Keep your eyes closed," I told the kid, but she'd felt the landing and the fresh air, and seemed intent on seeing her magical unicorn angel.

Her eyes grew big, all brown and fear, and a shriek ripped from her throat. Neighbors could be heard all around us now, several shouting about the backyard. And sirens blared in the distance.

Great. I mean, great for the kid. She was fine. Not so great for Clay and I.

"Bye bye," I told the kid, who still looked with terror at the purple-skinned demon girl who'd just saved her. I let her go, confident she was safe, and pulled the shadows to me and away from her. Clay stood not far away, and I folded the shadows around him, too. It required a bit more concentration but was easily enough done. Especially as several neighbors climbed up the fence to get to the girl.

"Let's go," he whispered, able to see me in the shadows. I nodded, looked back to the girl, and we jumped up the fence, into the next yard, and made our way back to the jail. Or school, as they insisted we call it.

Just as we jumped, I caught sight of my bush buddy, the flames traveling through the open windows and onto the next house, catching the wooden fence in their fury.

The bush stood silently, caught between burning homes, waiting to see if it would survive. Caught between fires, unable to escape, unable to change the course of its destiny…looking at that bush felt a bit like looking in a mirror.

And, just like myself, I couldn't figure out a way to save it.

2

___

WE SCRAMBLED BACK to the school, careful not to be seen. I kept the shadows around us, especially as we crossed well-lit roads where cars still sped about. I had a thousand questions to ask Clay.

What had happened in that house? Why had we gone there? How had he gotten knocked out? Who was that person who'd leapt into the second house? Why was the girl all alone? Could the bush survive the flames?

I glanced at him, but he had slipped into a funk and I was too tired to even voice my questions coherently. It had been a long night, and it was well past midnight. Tomorrow was a big day for both of us, and we had to get what little sleep we could.

We exited suburbia, slipped into a busy neighborhood which lined a manufacturing district.

The short houses drifted away and we were soon surrounded by tall buildings, shop fronts, neon lights and more life. I hooked my arm into Clay's, to keep the shadows tight around both of us. Fatigue etched the edges of my mind, making it more difficult for me to concentrate on keeping the shadows folded.

He glanced my way, concern lining his own fatigued eyes. I gave him a nod and quick grin. We didn't speak, for fear of being overheard. But he nodded back and focused on crossing the night crowd.

We knew of a nearby halfway house where Traded, aka people not of this world, aka people like us, could find safety for the night. But we were boarded Traded, and our school had strict rules of conduct. If we weren't in bed by the time morning checks were done, it would be noticed. And noted. And they'd know how to find us.

They always did. We knew *that* from experience.

I wished I'd had more time to look at the people around us. Sometimes, when Clay was too exhausted from a day of fighting or practice, I'd slip out of the school by myself to just hide in the shadows and watch people go by on this street. All types travelled this stretch, comfortable with who they were, as they talked and laughed, or fought and cried...I loved watching it all.

Being on the outskirts, and yet still feeling a part of it.

Some wore amazing clothing. And the shoes! The shoes were fabulous. I'd only ever had practical boots myself, but I hearted most of those shoes. Especially shiny heels. I had no clue if I could even walk in them, but I hoped to one day learn.

If I were given the chance. Tomorrow, or later today now, I suppose, they would give us our assignments. They would give us two weeks to get there. They'd kick us out of the only home most of us had known for the past thirteen years. And then they'd shutter it.

The whole prospect terrified me, and my grip on Clay's arm tightened. He felt the shift in my mood and placed his hand on mine, to comfort me.

What if Clay and I weren't going to the same guild? What if we were about to be separated forever? He was the only friend I'd had since coming to this world, and I didn't remember my other world. We'd met on the second day of school, after he'd saved me from some bullies, and we'd been fast friends ever since. I could count on Clay, and no one else. The very thought of losing him made my heart skip beats.

We crossed Beastwood Street and it was like stepping into a whole new world. The street lights vanished, the roads narrowed and became riddled with cracks, and a great expanse of forest rose all around, as though the city had given up.

But it hadn't given up. It was just too afraid to get

nearer to what loomed about two hours' walk away. We stuck to the trees, near the main road, the world all in shadows as though light feared this path. We walked in silence until our eyes caught a few yellow lights up ahead, surrounding our destination.

Like a monster from my darkest dreams, the old Harlington Penitentiary loomed ahead. Renamed the Margrave Academy, it still looked exactly like what it had been: a jail. Which made sense, because it essentially still functioned as one.

"One last time," Clay whispered. I nodded.

There was so much I wanted to say. About what his friendship had meant to me. How it had saved me so often from taking my own life, as so many others had. How he had been worth living for, and how the adventures and laughter had kept me going all these years.

I acutely feared that tomorrow would break us up, and that I might fold into shadows and never appear again. Because he'd not only made the light safe for a demon – he'd made it comfortable, even.

Best friends didn't really come in better packaging than he did, despite the brooding and secrets. I'd miss those, too.

I didn't say any of that. Instead, I followed him in silence as we climbed the outer wall, avoiding the lights. We separated just inside the jail, and he headed to his room (aka cell) while I headed to mine.

I wrapped the shadows more closely around myself as I watched him slip away and turn the corner.

Even though I was exhausted, sleep still proved elusive. Which is why I was still awake when the door (aka bars) to my room flew open. I sat up, wishing I had a weapon, ready to strike, but the tattoo on the side of my neck suddenly burned, and my energy drained out of me.

Damn it. I wished that thing didn't exist. It was some bio compound ink triggered by some tech kept by the teachers, or so a few students whispered. Maybe nanites. Maybe magic.

Who the hell knew.

Either way, it worked just fine, my head lolling back and forth as they grabbed my arms and dragged me down the corridor. A few students looked through their bars to see what was happening.

Great. What the hell had we done now? Well, I mean, I knew what we'd done. We weren't exactly supposed to sneak out of the school. But how had they found out? We'd done it often enough without being seen.

They dragged me downstairs, to a counselling room (aka interrogation room), and dropped me to the floor.

The tingling sensation around my neck stopped, and I could breathe easier. I pushed myself to a sitting position. The cold floor knocked me back to my senses. Two teachers (aka jailers) stood by the door, arms crossed. The door opened again, and Ms. Nadine stepped in. She wasn't super tall, but something about the way she held herself made her seem a lot taller. Not to mention intimidating.

"Ms. Misu," she said, the usual ice dripping from her voice. When I'd first arrived here, hoping to finally find a place where I was wanted, I'd really thought that Ms. Nadine's role was to be our surrogate mother. She kind of looked like one. Short gray hair curling around her soft face, slightly droopy eyes seeming always concerned, snow white skin lined with what I once believed to be laugh lines.

I'd since learned better.

They were definitely frown lines.

"Ms. Nadine," I said with as much politeness as I could muster as I forced myself to stand. Nadine did not take kindly to shows of disrespect. And whatever that thing on my neck was, she certainly had the ability to control it.

I stood well over a foot taller than her, but had no illusion that I could fight my way out of this. I stood with my arms at my side, as I'd been taught to do, and waited, biting the inside of my cheek.

She examined me for a moment. I was glad I'd taken the time to put on my blue cotton jumper (aka prison suit) before going to bed. It was against school rules to wear any fighting equipment outside of training.

And sneaking out of the school with Clay was

definitely not training. Well, not official training, anyway.

"You were outside earlier this evening," she finally said, her voice dripping with disappointment. I knew from experience that what she now expressed was much more dangerous than disappointment.

I wasn't sure what to say. We'd never been caught sneaking out before, or I'm sure we'd have been stopped from doing it again. How had she found out this time? And did they know about Clay?

And she hadn't technically asked a question. Really, she'd just made a statement.

"I want to give you the benefit of the doubt," she said, her voice softer than usual. I both wanted to flinch and ask for a hug. Any sign of gentleness from her and I was ready to forget years of torment to just find a soft place to land.

"Come with me," she said gently. I followed without question, the two jailers following close behind. I could take them, in a fair fight. I was faster and could hit hard. But it would never be a fair fight, so I didn't try, focusing on following Ms. Nadine instead.

We passed the other counselling rooms, and turned down a corridor. The barred doors were open, with guards on each side, each armed enough that it shattered the illusion that this was in fact a foster school for kids from another world.

I'd rarely been on this side of the school. I looked

around in curiosity at the offices and supply rooms. It almost made it seem normal. Instead of kids sleeping in jail cells separated by old cubicle walls, this was just a spot for admins and teachers to do their work, getting ready to help the kids succeed in the next steps of their careers.

The thought made me want to laugh, but that desire left me the second we turned left and I saw the man holding a little girl. The girl clung to her pink unicorn like it would save her.

I sighed. *Kids.* Couldn't she just accept that she'd been saved, instead of looking terrified and hiding in her dad's arms?

So I made a piss poor unicorn angel. I'd saved her ass anyway, hadn't I?

The father looked at me with poison in his eyes. I wanted to ask him where he'd been while his house burned down around his little girl. Had he been having an affair with a neighbor? Selling drugs? Not caring enough to protect the dreams of his child?

I took a step forward before I realized what I'd done, and a guard lurched towards me, his gun raised.

"Who did you see, child?" Ms. Nadine said, in that kind voice that I longed to hear used on me.

The little girl pointed at me and hid her face in her father's arm. I didn't know what those arms would do to her. I didn't know if they were kind or rough, loving or hateful. In my experience, most parents' arms hurt.

I didn't want the little girl to be hurt because I'd screwed up. I didn't want to lie, or even throw shade at the dad. I'd just wanted to be a unicorn angel for once.

"She's telling the truth," I whispered, keeping my voice low so as not to scare the child further. She'd already seen her house catch fire, knew demons now existed, would probably live in fear for the rest of her life. I didn't want to pile any more fears on her.

Ms. Nadine nodded to the dad, and said something to the child, in that voice that I now understood would never be directed my way. I lowered my head, looked down at the floor, and waited for the pain to hit my neck.

Once it did, I waited for the numbness I craved.

3

I STARED at the door in front of me. It was locked, of course, and made of reflective metal that just amplified the bright lights, each bulb well protected and like a dagger in my skin.

There was no bed. No desk. No chair. Not even a pillow. The ground was also reflective, making even the smallest of shadows nearly impossible.

I sat against the back wall, wrapped my arms around my knees, lowered my head into whatever shadows I managed to create this way. But it wasn't enough to make me feel safe.

There was no one here. I was alone, in a small cell, but I felt so exposed. Every bright light amplified the purple of my skin, the depth of my long dark hair, the horns sticking out of my scalp, and how *foreign* I was to this world. How I just didn't fit in. How its light didn't comfort me, but just scared me.

The door opened and I looked up, my tired mind not quite wrapping around what I saw. Clay stepped in, and the door closed behind him.

"Hey," he said as he crossed the whole six feet of the cell and knelt in front of me.

"Hey," I answered, squinting at him. "Did they catch you, too?"

He looked embarrassed. "No, they should have though. If that little girl hadn't seen you…"

"I'm glad she didn't see you," I whispered, and I lowered my head back into my arms, to hide the light. I could usually take more of it, especially when well rested. Some days it was just easier to face the light than others.

I glanced up again, regretting it as the light stabbed a migraine into my head. "What are you doing here?"

He shrugged. "Came to make sure you were okay. Word travels pretty fast."

"So they just let you in?" I asked incredulously.

This time, he grinned. "Jack's on duty."

I groaned. Jack and Clay had been tentative buddies, or at least allies, ever since Clay had caught Jack stealing some of the sedative supplies from the guard room, probably to sell on the streets. Clay had convinced Jack that he had evidence, even though he really didn't, and I was pretty sure Jack knew that. But for some reason, he put up with Clay's weird demands anyway.

No, maybe I understood why. Clay could be charming and funny. Hell, that's why I followed him into a thousand misadventures.

"Scooch," he said, and I squinted at him.

"Scooch?"

"Move over," he insisted, and I moved as far as I could, but the cell was four feet max in width.

He shifted beside me, and used his bigger frame to gather me up, hiding the lights from up above. "I should have brought a blanket," he mumbled.

"Your shadow helps," he wrapped his arms more tightly around me, shifted so that I had the corner, and covered as much of the light as he could. The heat from his body and the shadows he created soothed my growing headache, and I felt exhausted. Like all I had left to run on were fumes, and very few of them, at that.

"What were we doing tonight?" I asked.

Clay tensed up a bit, then relaxed. I'd never really asked about our capers. If there were goods or money to be split, he would. He always had.

"You trust me, right, Tira?" there was such a need in his voice that I wanted to reach out and hold him back, but didn't want to take my arms out from the safety of his shadow.

"I do," I said. And I meant it. "But I also want to

know what tonight was about. In case tomorrow we're separated." I was surprised I'd gotten the words out. I folded what shadows I could grab and pulled them more tightly around me, like a comfort blanket against the incoming harsh realities of this world.

Not of *our* world. Of *this* world.

The one we'd been stranded on. Traded with. Thousands of human babies switched up for monsters in their cradles, like fairy tales of old, nightmares made new. And so very real.

"I'm trying to keep us together," he said. "That was a try-out for a guild. For you and me. So we can get in the same one, you know?"

"You should have told me," I said, feeling a lump in my throat.

"I couldn't," he whispered. "Part of the deal. But, listen," his voice grew in strength. "I don't know that we failed. I don't really know what we were supposed to do."

I nodded, not convinced. Clay had been taken out. The house had burned down. The one inhabitant of that house had seen and identified me.

No, we'd failed. Tomorrow, after the graduation ceremony, we'd receive our invitations and be separated. Or worse, we'd receive no invitation and be cast as useless.

"I don't want to go to a circus guild," I said.

"You won't," Clay insisted. "I'll make sure of that."

I didn't think he could stop it. I didn't think he knew how, any more than I did, even though Clay actually spoke to people and made friends, and had contacts on the outside. Me? Not so much. People sucked and I preferred sticking with my own.

Clay was my own. That was it. And my world would be shrinking tomorrow. Until I found myself in a circus guild. Blake and the other bullies were right. What else could I realistically contribute to society, except to be a creature for people to fear in the night? To remind them that demons did exist and that you could be afraid of them for a reasonable entry fee?

My skin crawled with fear, my heart with fatigue.

"Thanks for trying," I said, letting myself fall further into the shadows that Clay created for me.

"Not giving up yet," he said, and I knew he meant it. But I also knew it probably wouldn't make a difference.

"I just want to go home," I said, not really knowing where home was. A home with others like me. Where the shadows were plentiful and full of comfort. Where I wasn't locked in a small reflective room with no shadows to cling to. Where I could walk down the street without being gasped at.

Where I could be a unicorn angel and save children without scaring them.

The home that I'd been stolen from, twenty years ago, presumably swapped out with a human baby who wanted to get back to their world just as badly as I wanted mine, even though they had no concept of their home. No more than I did.

Or that Clay did.

"I know," he said. "I'll get you there, someday."

That, I was willing to believe. Because there really was nothing else left to believe in. Clay was worth believing in, and I knew that he would do all that he could to find my home. And he'd follow me there, too, and make friends and contacts there. Just, be Clay. And I could be Tira.

Resolve strengthened me even as sleep enveloped me. I wouldn't be separated from Clay. I'd find a way to make sure we stayed together.

No matter what. Come hell or high water.

Oh, who was I kidding. Hell was already here.

Just not *my* hell.

4

WE ALL SAT PERFECTLY in our chairs, making sure to stay in line lest Ms. Nadine decided to correct our behavior. I sat near the end of a row, my hands practically twitching with impatience. I'd gotten some sleep thanks to Clay, who'd slipped out just before they came to collect me. I didn't know how rested he could be. He'd been awkwardly positioned to cover me with the shadows. But Clay's abilities didn't sap him like mine did. He mostly moved fast and punched damn hard.

Ms. Nadine called us to attention by simply walking onto the stage near the podium. I felt a bit better for having cleaned up and dressed in actual clothing before coming to the graduation ceremony (aka release day). I wasn't fooling myself into thinking it was a kindness. They just didn't want to keep me here longer than necessary, eager to ship me off to whatever guild or league, or more than likely circus, would have me.

I hated this useless pomp and circumstance. It dragged me out into the light for no good reason. I felt exposed and kept looking around me. I wasn't the only one here who couldn't pass as human at first glance, but my purple skin, long dark hair and, not to mention, the short horns sticking from my head, definitely marked me as *more* different.

Clay sat two rows ahead. Dressed all in black, he also stood out. His hair was longer than the school decreed, but they'd given up on trying to get him to respect this one piece of decorum. As though sensing my gaze, Clay glanced back and winked and grinned at me, making me feel instantly better. Or, at least, less alone.

"Now, for your valedictorian," Ms. Nadine said proudly, "Blake Connelly." Blake, blond hair perfectly coiffed, stepped on stage to give his speech. Clay glanced back my way again and rolled his eyes. I grinned.

Blake was a bully and a crass jackass. He'd only received the so-called honor because no one wanted to tell him he hadn't been selected.

I looked up at him, narrowing my eyes. Clay and Blake had pretty much declared each other lifelong enemies, after Blake had tried to steal Clay's pendant, the only thing Clay still had from back home.

Home. Real home. Not this fake one, on this strange planet. I wondered if Clay wanted to go home, too. He'd never mentioned it, only holding his pendant once in a while when we chatted about our future.

Maybe Clay didn't want to go to my home, even though he'd promised to get me there someday. Maybe he wanted to return to his own home, instead. And I got that completely. I knew without a doubt that I'd help him reach that goal, just as he'd help me reach mine. But the day suddenly seemed a lot colder at the thought that we couldn't just be together on any world.

Anyway, all of this thinking was useless. I'd end up in a circus guild within two weeks, guaranteed. It's not like there was any way to get back home. They still didn't know what the hell had happened twenty years ago, and a demon and a fighter weren't going to be the ones to crack that mystery.

"This place has been our home for more than a decade," Blake droned on. He looked human, which made me dislike him even more. The divide between human and Traded was clear, sure, but even the Traded had lines drawn between them. Those who could pass as human, and those who couldn't.

I certainly couldn't. I'd tried, once, with makeup. The stuff was so thick it had cracked when I smiled. And I'd missed the purple sheen of my skin.

I liked the purple. Plus, wearing a silly hat to hide my horns had looked ridiculous.

Clay could pass as human, if he cared to. His teeth were a bit too sharp, though, and his hands more like claws. But, if he brooded instead of smiled, which he usually did when he wasn't trying to cheer me up, he could pass as a grouchy human.

Except, if you stared too long at his dark eyes, you could feel yourself drawn into them in a way that was definitely not human.

Blake? You could stare at him all day and all you'd see is a pretty boy. I wouldn't be surprised if he joined a performers guild.

"Today, we step out into the world, waiting to greet us with open arms…"

His speech was as bland as he was. And he was an idiot if he believed that. The world didn't want to greet us with open arms. The world wanted us gone. It couldn't keep us forever in these schools, but it didn't want us on the streets, either.

"In the two weeks gifted to us as we make our way to our future," I tried not to snort at him. Did he really believe all of that? This wasn't a future. This wasn't a career.

Boring Blake was also Stupid Blake.

"I know that I, for one, intend to be a force for good out there."

This time, I failed to hold back my snort. Blake heard me. Hell, the whole gymnasium heard me, and they were all turning to look at the demon girl. I was sure my purple was growing deeper, but Clay covered for me, starting to cough snort.

Everyone laughed, and Blake turned bright red, staring with dark eyes at Clay and I. Not that that was unusual. He'd always hated us. After today, we'd hopefully never have to see him again.

That would be one good thing about leaving this place. One of many. This place didn't exactly hold fond memories. Nothing did, really, except for a few friends. But I don't really have many of those, either.

"*Some* of us will make a good difference out there," he spat out. I rolled my eyes at Clay. It had taken him that long to come back with an insult, and that was the best he could do. Ms. Nadine glared at Clay and me, though, so we returned to our best behavior.

The tattoo on my neck began to tingle. I was sure Clay's did, too. The school didn't technically have to give us two weeks. Lots of kids were going to be leaving in the old yellow school buses lining the front of the school, to head directly to their guilds. Not all of the destinations were near, after all.

I didn't think they'd be given two weeks to explore. More like two weeks to learn the ropes to be ready to do whatever was expected of them on opening night.

Opening night. A lump formed in my throat just thinking about it. About the spotlight, trained on you, the shadows deserting you...I couldn't go to a circus guild.

I was terrified. I wondered if what Clay said was true. It might be. That maybe once we left here, we'd be able to join a guild together. Whatever that test was, maybe it was something we'd passed.

Please let there be an invitation in my room. Please let it be for the same guild as Clay. Please give us two weeks together if not, and don't just send us away on a school bus.

Just another few minutes and we'd be free, and the school shut down. It wasn't like there were multiple cohorts of this class. One bunch of Traded, from one moment, twenty years ago. Traded all from different worlds, as far as we could tell, thousands of worlds across stretches unknown.

This school would shut down, and we'd become something else. Something that contributed to society in whatever way this society, still grieving its missing children and fearing the monsters that had replaced them, decided we could best contribute.

The rest of Blake's speech didn't register at all. I was too busy thinking about what I would do out there. I really didn't know. I didn't know which guild would welcome me, and where I would feel useful.

It'd be nice to at least not be feared and hated.

It seemed like a little ask, but when you looked like a demon, it was the only ask you ever truly had.

FOLLOWING MORE platitudes and haughty airs, Ms. Nadine finally took the stage again. Blake took his seat, near mine. He cast a dark glance my way, but I ignored him.

With any luck, he'd be gone right after the ceremony, off to join whatever league or organization would have him. Hopefully far from where I'd end up.

"Over the past few years," Ms. Nadine began, "we tried to instill you with a sense of belonging."

I tried really hard not to scoff again. I somehow managed it, and grinned as Clay shuffled in the seat ahead, imagining he fought the same battle as me.

"And, as you step out, remember your place." She paused, looked at each of us in turn. I could swear she stopped longer on me, but that might just have been the nerves.

"Some of you will step out into a pre-selected place, with offers awaiting you back at your rooms." The selected few, sure. We'd seen the guild leaders ramping up for our cohort. The guilds were created specifically to keep us occupied. All of us, across various schools and holding places around the world. I didn't know how many, or where exactly they were. That's not something they'd taught us in civics class.

Instead, they'd taught us about the values of human society, while teaching us to fight and protect ourselves, to get us ready to join various guilds.

A place to live, to work, to be useful members of

society. To serve important roles without humans having to worry about us being around them.

Practically indentured servitude.

"Those of you who don't receive an invitation, you'll need to select one before your two weeks are up." She smiled, as though encouraging us to consider the possibilities. "Above all," she concluded, "remember that, once in your guild, you are there for life. And may those years be as productive to society as possible."

To human society. That part wasn't stated, but it was certainly implied.

A scattering of applause echoed in the gym. Blake was loudest among them, getting more to rally with his dark looks. I sighed and didn't bother, crossing my arms and waiting to be dismissed.

Finally the moment came. Without further ado, Ms. Nadine nodded and stepped off the stage. We looked around, but the teachers were exiting. It was over. We were free to leave the school.

I stood, feeling numb. This was the moment Clay and I had talked about for so long. The moment of us receiving invitations to the same guild.

We began filing out of the gymnasium. The air crackled with nervous energy. Everyone was anxious to get back to their room and find out if an invitation was waiting for them.

Clay fell in step with me.

"Where you wanna go after this?" he asked.

"Not sure," I said, finding comfort in his stubborn belief that we'd be fine. "I guess it depends on if we have guild offers?" I gave him a wry smile, which he returned

"I'm not worried," he shrugged.

The students filed out toward the rooms, some speaking excitedly, others quiet. I looked around, wondering if we'd ever get a moment like this again. Of everyone around us being from another world. Of finding comfort in the fact that we were all Traded, and none of us belonged on this planet.

As soon as we left this place, we were going to be sharing space with humans. Some of us would blend in fine. But not all of us.

"Meet you up front?" Clay said. I nodded, and we parted ways. Our rooms were in different wings. They just stuffed us in as they found us, so we didn't exactly get to pick. The one thing I did like about this place was that you got your own room. Not that that was super impressive once you realized old jail cells had been repurposed for holding us. Still, everyone got a small room, a toilet and a sink. And the ability to be kept in lockdown if we didn't behave.

After last night, I wouldn't miss this place at all. Just thinking about that solitary confinement made me shudder.

Clay was right. We'd find better out there.

A smile crept onto my lips, as I remembered past

capers and started to allow myself to hope for new ones. The traffic grew thinner, the students all filing away into their own cells. I heard some excited shouts around me, but very few. There were moans, and silence.

That silence bothered me most. I focused on the memories, a smile still on my lips as I turned into my cell.

"Got lots to smile about there, demon?" Blake's voice resonated behind me. My smile soured and I only half turned.

"Getting away from you gives me plenty to smile about," I shot back. He snorted.

"That was some stunt you pulled off. Here I thought you hated bringing attention to yourself."

He was coming closer, and I turned to face him fully. He blocked the exit to my cell. *Great.* If the boy wanted a fight, he'd have it. Biggest problem was that I didn't actually know what Blake could do. He kept that close to his chest, so I'd learned to always be cautious around him. He had a reputation you didn't mess around with. Especially since a few of his "enemies" happened to just vanish.

I stood my ground nonetheless. He glanced at my wall. They used old cubicle walls, mostly gray, to give us some privacy between cells. It made it even smaller, but at least it made it ours.

"No invitation, I see?" he smirked and held up a

piece of paper between his hands. It was gold-rimmed and looked damn fancy. Of course.

"Did they invite you to the Dickheads R Us Guild?"

Oh wow. Even I was embarrassed by how bad that comeback was.

He took another step toward me. I continued to stand my ground, though shifted my right leg slightly, ready to move if he attacked. I was pretty sure that I was faster than him, but not sure enough to strike first.

"I won't forget what you did today," he said, all dark and evil like, and then smirked, like he was going to lean down and kiss me. But he didn't, turning around instead, and vanished around the corner.

I hadn't realized that I'd been holding my breath. As soon as he'd been gone long enough for me to be sure that he wasn't coming back, I started to breathe again. Damn Blake. I wouldn't miss that guy one bit.

Or this place. I didn't have much to bring with me. Mementos were few, as my "adoptive family" had dumped me here the first chance they got. Hadn't seen them since. Didn't really mind that part. They had been terrible, and I hoped that their own kid, the one that probably ended up in my crib in a faraway world, had found a nicer, kinder family.

I liked to think she had.

I threw my clothing in my backpack and looked around for something else to take, but I didn't have anything of value or worth keeping. I hoped to change that out in the world.

I turned when something caught my eye. A black barrette lay on my pillow, one of those fancy (to me, anyway) hair pieces. I had a regular elastic that I used to braid my hair during practice. That was it. I'd never even seen a barrette in person before.

I looked around me, my devil tail swishing in distrust. No one was here, and I couldn't see any sign of anyone having been here. Then again, it wasn't like this place was super secure. It was mostly just good at keeping people in.

I took a closer look. The design was simple and delicate. When turned at a forty-five degree angle to the light, a figure eight, an infinity symbol, revealed itself, carefully etched in the barrette's strange material.

There was no note attached to it.

Who the hell had left it here?

The bell rang again, giving us our ten-minute warning. They really wanted us out. The faculty would probably breathe easier once we were gone.

But would the world? That part, I didn't know. I had no idea how they'd prepped for us, if at all. They'd shut most of us out for years. I doubted a warm welcome waited for us on the other side. Maybe those two weeks to reach our guilds were to test that out. Limited-time offer for the Traded to prove they could in fact live among humans and not necessarily be trapped in guilds.

That would be nice. The chance to actually have options.

"Ready to go?" Clay popped into my room, turning sideways to clear the entrance. I slipped the barrette into my backpack and, with barely a glance back, I followed him out of the jail cell that had served as my room for the past thirteen years.

"I really am," I whispered to the shadows I left behind.

WE CLEARED a few groups of hugging students. I caught snippets of conversations, mostly exclamations at where they were headed next.

Some organizations, some businesses, even, but mostly guilds and leagues. The guilds. Strange and shady constructs with the sole purpose of keeping track of us. Of making sure we stayed in line.

Most students were showing off invitations (more like orders to join) from various guilds. I spotted a few disappointed faces, though. The ones not selected now had two weeks to convince a guild to take them on. I wasn't clear on what would happen if one of us didn't have a placement by then.

Probably best not to find out.

We stepped out of the building. The yard stretched before us, leading to a now-open gate at the end. It was a good sight. Still, I glanced right and left, not quite believing we were just going to be allowed to walk out.

A few students walked ahead, and Clay grinned at me.

"Shall we?" he asked, and we practically bounced down the steps and walked up the path. We paused just before stepping out.

"Haven't been out of here, in the daylight, in thirteen years," Clay said. I'd never heard him sound even remotely wistful beforehand.

"Did you get a guild invitation?" I knew he wasn't going back to his foster family, no more than I was. Clay's mom was dead, and he'd never mentioned a dad, so I assumed he didn't have one. Or not one worth mentioning.

"Did you?" he asked. I thought about the barrette, but that wasn't an invitation. Maybe a gift, I guess, though I couldn't figure out who'd bother. I hadn't exactly made many friends.

"No," I shrugged. "Their loss."

He grinned my way. "Just you and me, then?"

I felt instant relief, all the stress oozing out of my tense muscles. "Guess so! I told you we failed that test."

He nodded and looked serious. "Spectacularly. We failed it *spectacularly*."

I laughed. "Yes. But we made it out, right? Because we watched each other's backs."

"Always," he said. "But, like, it was *very* spectacular."

"I told the girl I was a unicorn angel, Clay."

He glanced my way. "Oh ya? What's that even like?"

"I don't know, but she didn't seem to think I fit the bill."

"Hey, if you want to be a unicorn angel, Tira, then you be a unicorn angel."

I laughed again, feeling free for the first time in, well, ever. "So, where to now? We have to find something within two weeks. What the hell do we do before then?"

"Well," Clay said, "I guess we can head into one of the fine in-city halfway houses offered to us while we interview at guilds."

I glanced at his backpack, and my equally small pack of possessions. I raised an eyebrow at him. "Are we supposed to dress up for this interview?"

"I doubt they're hiring us for our wardrobe," Clay said, a note of bitterness in his voice.

"No," I agreed, and then added, "it'll definitely be for our good looks."

He laughed, and the temporary damper on his mood seemed to have lifted.

"Shall we?" he said, offering his arm. I took it and we crossed the threshold of the school grounds and stepped into the new day.

Buses, vans, cars and even a few limos passed us by as we walked down the road toward the city. Some guilds and businesses had offered positions to multiple students, the buses loud and full as they sped by. Some parents and families had come to pick up their kids and celebrate the happy occasion of their graduation.

Go figure.

One of the circus buses rumbled past with darkened windows, but I saw a few familiar faces in some of the opened windows, non-human eyes and features looking my way. I couldn't shake the sadness behind the lack of enthusiasm I read in their eyes. They didn't even get two weeks of freedom, shipped right away to who knows how far away.

Part of me couldn't believe I hadn't received an

invitation to a circus guild. Best not think too much about it, and just be grateful it hadn't happened.

The dust from the buses dissipated and I noticed that Clay had pulled up his hood despite the relative warmth of the day. I knew that move. He felt overwhelmed, though he'd never admit it. Clay liked adventures, and a good fight, but he hated uncertainty. Plus, I'd managed to get some sleep, but only because he'd sacrificed his.

"Let's walk through the forest," I offered, and headed toward the shade of the bordering trees. By the time we'd reach the road again, the buses should all be past. Not to mention the cars carrying the happy families.

It was one thing being on the outside looking in, but when you'd essentially just been kicked out of the only place that had been your home for more than a decade, you didn't need the reminder that you no longer had one.

And that no one else wanted you to be a part of their family, either.

We went a ways into the trees, Clay seeming to relax a bit more.

Still, we didn't share a word, and his hood stayed up. I followed in silence, respecting his space, heading toward the only place I knew for sure would be safe for us this night.

As soon as we stepped out of the forest and crossed

Beastwood Drive, I folded every nearby shadow around me. The light posts provided some, and the nearby factories. Clay automatically moved closer to me and I wrapped him in my shadows, too.

We'd walked non-stop for almost three hours before reaching our destination, behind the industrial sector, near the main drag. We were in an older area of town with dilapidated buildings, drug deals happening on several corners. The cops didn't care enough to be around. And there was the Traded halfway house, waiting for us.

I'd never really been in a halfway house before. My foster family, although they didn't like me (aka feared me), made sure to keep a roof over my head and kept tabs on me. And then, once I'd been shipped off to the Margrave Academy, I'd never seen them again. But some of the Traded that I'd met at the schools had spent some of their time in these halfway houses, after being rejected by foster families and having little other recourse. These places were deemed safe, and Traded could legally be here, as long as they were heading toward a school or, now, I suppose a guild.

The building was in an alleyway, away from human sight. It wasn't even named, the sign above the door simply saying "Traded Post." A second big sign had been added to the front of the house— *Closing in Two Weeks to Traded. Present Proof. Join Your Guild or Group Now. That's the Law.*

"Well, that's friendly," I mumbled. Clay opened the door and stepped in.

A desk greeted us, which used to be a bar, pretty sure. No one stood behind it. This was probably a dive bar repurposed years ago. That would explain at least some of the stale, musty smell. I approached as Clay lowered his hood to take in our surroundings.

A note had been left. *Find a bed. Don't make a mess.*

"Straightforward enough."

We headed past the curtained door, to the sleeping area. Bunk beds lined both sides of the room, leaving only a few feet as a passageway in between. All in all, about forty people could sleep here, though certainly not comfortably. The bathrooms waited at the end of the corridor. Without seeing them, I could smell them.

"The beds look clean at least," I mumbled and threw my bag on one. Clay took the one beside it and he grunted.

"Gonna go clean up," he said and shuffled toward the back, vanishing into the men's bathroom. I stretched and stared at the few posters on the walls. The city's aquarium. The amusement park. All marked as Traded friendly.

A smile tugged at my lips at the memory of the school trips they used to organize for us. I used to love them, as long as they let me keep my hood up. Which they usually did, to save themselves some trouble. But then Clay got caught on one of his little outings and was held back from further trips. I'd stayed with him, to keep him company.

I didn't care about seeing the damn aquarium or sad amusement park one more time. I just hadn't wanted my friend to be left alone in solitary.

Sorry. They called it "Time Out."

I sighed, my tail whisking angrily behind me at the memories. Of Clay trapped there before. Of me thrown in there last night…but we weren't there anymore. We were actually free. My tail drooped as I wrapped my head around that concept. We didn't have to be *anywhere*.

We had no deadline or curfew. I mean, we had two weeks to place ourselves within a guild since we hadn't received any offers, but we had *two weeks*. Two weeks of basically unsurveilled freedom. In a crappy halfway house, sure, but right now it looked like we had the run of the place.

That was damn nice.

"You're looking pretty serious over there," Clay yawned as he joined me again, water dripping from his hair.

I grinned, still feeling elated. "Two weeks," I said. "We have an entire two weeks without having to report to anyone!"

Clay grunted noncommittally.

I raised an eyebrow.

"What?" I asked. He shot me another, much smaller

grin. I groaned. He sat down on the bed in front of me. "What did you do?"

He shrugged, his dark eyes focusing on mine, some of his hair falling across them. Clay had never met a comb he liked, or a haircut he enjoyed, so he'd kind of given up. I could convince him to let me cut some of his hair off, but I doubted I had a great future as a hairdresser.

I raised my second eyebrow.

"Well," he started casually. I knew that tone. He was trying to downplay something. "I might have a gig for us tonight, if you're in. It's a doozy."

If I had a third eyebrow, I'd have raised that, too. I'd never heard him call any gig a "doozy" before. That didn't bode super well.

"What's the gig?" I asked, still eyeing him suspiciously. If he noticed my glare, he was a pro at ignoring it. A rat ran in, stopped, took one look at me, and took off immediately. At least someone took my glares seriously.

"Well, here's the thing," he said. I groaned. I knew those words well. They were usually padding words for anything he thought I wouldn't quite approve of. "I'm not exactly sure what the gig is. Not yet!" He quickly added.

"That doesn't sound like a really super smart idea," I offered, trying to keep my voice level.

"Buuttt," he added, apparently enjoying my reaction.

I'd try to hit him, but knew I'd never land the blow. He grinned, as though reading my mind.

He was really enjoying this. Who was I kidding? There was no way I wouldn't follow along.

I sighed.

"I'm in," I said.

He nodded, as though he hadn't expected anything else. I kinda liked that. The more things changed, the more I could count on Clay to keep things interesting.

6

THE SHADOWS ENVELOPED me as I stepped into them, like an old friend greeting me. I glanced around my surroundings, trying to spot where Clay was hiding. I'd scouted my end of the street, and it had been clear. This time, we weren't trapped in boring suburbia, but instead in the industrial sector of town.

I was excited that the walk back to the halfway house was so short. It was like having a shorter work commute all of a sudden!

I still wasn't sure what the target was, except that it was a container of some sort. Clay hadn't been wrong in his assessment that his would be a doozy. Our information was sparse, at best. We would apparently know the target when we saw it, because it would look like a cylinder with a screw top and some hazard stickers (love those), and it would be small enough to carry.

I wish Clay had asked about the hazard stickers, but he was sure it wouldn't be a problem.

He was probably right, as long as we kept the container sealed. The fact that the client had no idea if the warehouse would be guarded or not would probably be a bigger problem, anyways. At least they'd equipped us. Guns and blades were the name of the game, which made me feel a lot happier. I hadn't handled a weapon since the last training session at school, almost a week ago! All of the weapons strapped around me were black, too. The shadows were thick, the night dark, my entire attire equally midnight-hued, so I barely wrapped the shadows around me to hide. Even if I unsheathed one of my swords, they wouldn't see the blade glinting. Not until I cut them, anyway.

My breathing sped up with excitement, and I forced it to slow down so that I remained focused.

I spotted Clay across the way, crouching low, keeping to the shadows himself. He headed towards the back of what seemed to be an old brick warehouse or industrial building of some sort. It seemed out of place among the newer metal constructions.

He headed for the right side door and I followed, dropping the shadows so he could see me. We'd agreed on a quick recon, and that we'd stick together. He'd argued against it at first, but reminding him that he'd been knocked out last night had helped my case.

He pulled the door open with some force, but no alarm sounded. Our intel was right on that end. It could mean poor security, or security that didn't rely on outside help. The potential of the latter promised more fun.

We stepped into a vast empty space, a few cars and vans strewn about, though no markings noted which company they represented. The space was clean and looked new, despite the outdated exterior. And even though it looked disorganized and haphazard, I couldn't help but feel like there was some pattern at play here, something that I couldn't quite pick up at a glance.

I followed Clay, clutching a handgun, my senses on high alert. The air didn't smell stale like I'd expected from an abandoned warehouse. It smelled like metal, and maybe some recent exhaust. I could even detect an undercurrent of cleaning materials, mostly bleach.

Somebody definitely used this place regularly.

There was no sign of anyone right now, though. It was late, which might explain its emptiness, but I still kept up my guard.

I glanced up and perused the walls, looking for security cameras and alarm systems. Nothing jumped out at me. We reached the back of the warehouse. An open door greeted us. Easy for an ambush.

Of course.

Clay grinned at me from the other side of the door. Adrenaline pumped my limbs to life.

He moved toward the door, but I held up my hand. I'd go first. My chances of going undetected were a lot better than his. He nodded, though I could see he didn't like it. I gave him a wry smile and winked. If I got in trouble, he could charge in to help me.

I wrapped the shadows around me. Clay stopped looking my way and focused on the door, so I knew he could no longer see me.

I took a deep breath, then moved quickly around the corner, holding my Glock 22 in front of me. Pretty standard gun fare, even a little bit dull. But pretty easy to come by, so I wasn't surprised we'd been supplied with it.

The next room was dark, even darker than the one I'd just stepped out of. I didn't turn around, but could feel that Clay had followed me.

I glanced back at Clay and wrapped my shadows around him. He gave me a quick look with another rueful grin. I squinted to try to get a better look at my surroundings. I could see a desk directly in front of me, and beyond it, another door.

Another funnel. How could I be liking this less and less, while enjoying it more and more?

I nodded to Clay and we moved forward, proceeding on each side of the desk. He needed to leave the safety of my shadows, but he was careful and quiet. We'd almost cleared the desk before I stopped and dropped my shadows so that Clay could see me and, more importantly, so that he could see my puzzled look.

There was nothing on the other side of the desk. Not even a chair. That was weird, and I didn't think weird was good.

The door in front of us wasn't open this time. A closed door seemed much worse.

Clay had pulled out his favorite hand-axe, which reflected no light. He shifted it in his hand. I knew from having seen it in action that it was sharp. The fact that he'd selected that weapon told me that he didn't know if he'd be fighting in close quarters, or if he'd be throwing it.

I debated switching out my weapon, but I could fire a shot at close range, too, and quickly grab a sword from there.

Clay indicated that he would be the one to turn the handle, in case it was booby trapped. This part I hated —this constant Russian roulette of "that might blow up" or "this might be triggered" or "this might be alarmed," and my least favorite: "Let me take this hit." But that's why we travelled as a pair. Just in case one of us got knocked out or taken out—the other could drag them out. Our last heist was proof of concept.

He pushed the door open. It didn't even creak, but

in the silence I managed to find my breath again. We moved forward and stepped in at the same time as I gathered the shadows around us. I held my gun out before me to clear the way, Clay's hand-axe ready to be thrown, or to block a blow.

Nobody attacked, but the place stank unlike anything I'd ever smelled before. And I'd smelled death more than once.

Clay shot me a grin. I holstered my gun. The thought of a giant bang echoing across the entire warehouse worried me about as much as Clay's enthusiasm. I pulled out a couple of throwing knives, silent but deadly. As long as my opponent's armor wasn't too thick, anyways.

I squinted to look more deeply into the warehouse. The darkness stretched far beyond us, but this darkness seemed different. I couldn't quite pierce it with my eyes, which was definitely strange. I looked towards Clay. He looked back my way, and we shared a quick nod. The glint of incoming battle still shone in his eyes. But the restraint of not wanting to get either one of us killed would keep him near me, at least. That was something.

We took another step forward, separating to cover more ground. I dropped the shadows again. Having Clay able to see me was more advantageous than having one of us hidden.

As we walked further into the room, the stench seemed to dissipate.

I turned around, curious to see if I could spot the origin of the stench. At first I couldn't see anything, but then the wall beside the door shimmered, dull metal rippling and cracking to form muscle. Not skin, unfortunately.

Just muscle. Raw, red, icky muscle.

The creature stepped forward, those muscles stinking like rotten meat.

I gagged and took a step back, as did Clay.

The creature, a Traded, I had to assume, stood six and a half feet tall, and was wider than the door. No blood dripped from their sinewy muscles, which wrapped around their entire form. Whatever this thing was, they certainly looked less human than most Traded did. But that didn't mean we weren't on the same team, either.

"Hey," I shot a grin their way, "nice to meet you."

Clay groaned.

The creature's mouth stretched apart, revealing sharp teeth, the lips not clearly defined against the traffic jam of muscle. I found some comfort in the muscle pattern, which didn't look human. It's not like if you could just take a human, strip off the skin, and get this creature, because even that would look different. Not, of course, that I had taken the skin off anyone. But I'd certainly seen it done.

I waited for a few seconds, but no answer came. They didn't move to stop us, either, just kind of standing between us and the door, their feet slightly separated, one behind the other. I think they'd cross their arms if they could, but part of me imagined that they would just kind of stick together with muscle goo.

I tried not to let the disgust show on my face. That wouldn't be super polite. I also tried really hard not to look down past their waist.

"Tira," Clay whispered.

I turned slightly to look at what he indicated. An orange light had been lit at the back of the warehouse. It seemed to cast no light beyond its predefined borders, but it served as a beacon.

Which begged the question: a beacon for what?

"What kind of a gig was this again?" I asked Clay.

"Just follow my lead," he said, shooting a disarming grin my way. I couldn't help but notice that he hadn't answered my question.

I really needed to start joining him for gig negotiations.

7

CLAY PRACTICALLY VIBRATED with excitement the closer we came to that orange light. I grew more and more suspicious, squinting into the light that seemed intent on blinding us. I glanced away from it, trying to avoid spots in my vision.

Was that movement movement beside us in the darkness? I resisted the urge to fold the shadows around me. If we'd already been spotted, they hadn't attacked yet. And they could get in an attack before I vanished, especially because I'd try to drag Clay in, too.

I could hear small scuffing sounds near us.

I reached out and placed my hand on Clay's arm, afraid that he'd missed the obvious in his excitement to reach that orange light and whatever it represented. To his credit, he slowed down and turned my way. He nodded, barely perceptible, acknowledging that something was up.

The orange light seemed to become impatient at our slowed progress, growing in intensity. Clay's eyes glowed with it, the strange quality of his irises capturing the brightness and holding it prisoner. He turned to me and grinned, sharp teeth glistening.

"What are we doing?" I whispered to Clay, although my whisper seemed to resonate across the entire hall.

"Trust me," he said. I arched an eyebrow. He'd been saying that a lot today.

He looked more closely at the orange light. I wanted to turn and face the darkness, but found myself drawn to the light as well. I thought it had been some kind of LED something-or-other, as everything seemed to be, but no. It was actually a very tiny person. A fairy, maybe? Did those exist? Everything seemed to exist now that the Traded were here. I mean, I was pretty much a demon, so why couldn't fairies exist?

Whatever kind of fairy this was, it didn't look super friendly. Its limbs were short and chunky, attached to its round, luminescent body. Its wings looked sharp, their darkness absorbing the light emanating from its body. The creature was three inches tall, tops. It was completely naked so that its luminescence could be fully seen. It looked at us, quite annoyed.

"You're late," it hissed.

Clay shrugged. "Your instructions were less than obvious," he said.

I glanced from Clay to the creature. Was this Clay's contact? All of this time, had all of our heists been ordered by a small orange lightbulb with wings?

Before I could stop it, I snorted out laughter. Clay groaned. The creature looked at me, its glow increasing. All except its eyes, which darkened—two round, black pupils centered perfectly on its head.

Really, if I thought about it, it kind of looked like an ugly luminescent snowman. I lowered my head so I would stop looking at it. I was going to laugh again, and I didn't think it was taking it kindly.

"Is something funny, Ms. Misu?"

Well, sure, something is funny, I wanted to say, but I didn't, in a moment of rare wisdom. I tried to collect my thoughts, or at least stop laughing. I closed my eyes, pinched the bridge of my nose, took a deep breath.

I looked back up.

Nope, too early. I cracked a smile. Thank goodness Clay stepped in to save me.

"She starts laughing when she gets nervous or excited for a fight," he said. I pictured fighting this thing and squashing it, and quickly covered my snort with a cough.

"Look," I said, trying to be useful, although perhaps failing, "it's really distracting to me right now that the only thing I'm looking at is you, a tiny little orange lightbulb. So do you want to give us more light so I know exactly who's creeping at the edges of this light? Because that would be okay. If we're going to fight, let's do this. If you want to do it in darkness, that's fine, but you're the first thing I'm coming after."

I straightened up and shook out my arms, the adrenaline of incoming battle flowing through me. I wasn't sure if Clay was going to be mad at me or amused. His grin quickly told me that he was more on the amused side. But his back was too stiff for casual amusement, and his fingers practically twitched around the hilt of his axe. Clay was nervous—which meant this was going to be a lot more dangerous than I'd hoped.

"Very well," the creature hissed. It hovered for a few moments, its wings not moving, then exploded in a little shower of sparks. I half-gasped and half-laughed at the show, until those sparks exploded outward, creating a firmament of orange stars around us, which all gathered together to cast light across the entire room.

"Oh," I said, standing back-to-back with Clay, automatically reaching for my silk-thin katana, grabbing my Glock with the other hand.

Clay tensed beside me, his reaction unfamiliar. Usually he relaxed his muscles right before a fight, but not now. I turned his way, feeling my jubilance at the upcoming battle die a tiny bit. This wasn't what he'd expected.

He still held his axe in one hand and pulled out a nasty-looking serrated blade in the other. He was going for close combat, which made sense. We were surrounded, and not just a little bit. There were at least twenty people around us. They were definitely Traded, of all different types. One of them had muscles which seemed to snake below the surface. Another had long legs and short arms, and very sharp teeth. Practically the entire rainbow was represented here in skin tones. My purple skin fit right in!

One of the Traded lifted a glowing orange arm, and I yelped as a stream of fire shot my way. I stumbled to the ground, cursing. They'd effectively separated Clay and I.

Now, that I didn't like. I moved back to the left, trying to regain my ground with Clay, but he'd been engaged by two nasty-looking enemies—one fuzzy, one not—that was as far as I got analyzing them before I was defending myself.

I shot at the Traded flamethrower—a satisfying scream welcoming my efforts. Claws swept down to take a chunk out of my arm and I moved down and to my right, kicking out and knocking down a green attacker.

I really did love all of these colors. But I didn't love

how quickly he got back up, using a large tail to push off the ground and regain his footing.

Clay shifted sideways, trying to get close to me, and I did the same, folding every shadow in the room around myself and Clay. My attacker's eyes grew wide as he pulled his claws back, not certain where I'd gone. I took advantage of that, slicing down with my katana and taking off one of his hands. He yowled in pain as blue blood flowed from his wound.

Clay's back pressed against mine, and this was suddenly a lot more fun. We shifted, still in my shadows. We were surrounded, but they wouldn't see our hits coming. I heard two thumps behind me, sheathed my gun and threw two knives to take out two more fighters.

Gunshots were too easy to track.

Clay grunted and stumbled. My blood ran cold. He'd taken a hit. I pulled the shadows closer, but there was nowhere to go, even if they couldn't tell where we were. They surrounded us.

Two more walked forward, one toward me, and I glanced back to see one more heading toward where Clay should be, though he'd dodged left as he quickly patched the wound on his arm.

I realized that they weren't trying to swarm us. They were methodical, probably trying to tire us out, to finish us off slowly.

"I can smell blood!" a short pinkish blob screamed from the back. That wasn't good.

The orange lightbulb, which I should have squashed, flickered on and off, and eradicated the shadows enough that our protective barrier vanished. I tried folding them back, but the light flickered again.

That was definitely not good.

"Damn it," I whispered, then shot a wide grin to the few Traded facing me, now quite able to see me. A few took a step back. I gripped my weapons loosely, ready for the attack.

"Get 'em, Barbara!" one of the remaining Traded screamed.

"Barbara?" I snorted.

Barbara stepped forward, all height, muscles and anger, with bright yellow skin and pink hair. I wasn't actually sure of their gender, but that hardly mattered. What mattered was the giant hammer that they swung down toward my head. I leapt back and knocked into Clay. He steadied himself, making sure I didn't fall, while the hammer came within an inch of striking my nose.

I pulled out two more throwing knives, flicking them directly at Barbara's face. Barbara, it turned out, had skin that was impenetrable by my throwing knives. They just bounced off and fell uselessly to the floor.

They grinned at me as I stood there panting, unarmed.

"Great…" I mumbled. "I think we should get out of here," I said to Clay as I avoided another blow, pulling him to the left a tiny bit so that he wouldn't get smacked from behind.

"I don't think we can," he breathed heavily as he parried and returned blows of his own. I busied myself trying to avoid Barbara's various glorious and angry attacks.

"Look, I didn't mean to insult your name!" I said as I threw two knives directly at their eyes. Their blinking might give us enough time to move. But the smoke bomb would definitely give us our escape route. I yelped, our usual signal so Clay wouldn't be caught unaware, and threw down a round vial, smoke quickly exploding out and filling the area. A great resource for failing shadows.

I grabbed Clay's arm. Time to run toward the exit, find our way while everybody coughed and tried to recover their senses.

Usually we'd be running like hell by now. But this time, Clay held back. He didn't move with me. And in that split second it took for me to try to figure out what he was up to, and how to pull him after me, a blow struck me on the side of the head. His arm slipped from my grip, and I couldn't find it again.

It wasn't the best feeling in the world to slip into darkness with.

8

THE FIRST THING that tugged at the edges of my consciousness was the smell. No—smell was too kind a word for this. This was a *stench*. A downright stink.

And it wasn't *just* a stench. It was a miasma. Like some kind of dark cloud created with the sole purpose of lining my lungs and nose with putridness.

My head hurt. That was the second thing that caught my attention. A dull throb in the back of it. I couldn't quite feel the rest of my body yet. That had been a good blow, but I was still alive. Something to celebrate, I suppose.

Clay…*where was Clay?*

My eyes shot open and I groaned. There was just enough light to jab into my pupils and stab my brain directly.

I swore. Then moaned.

The stench intensified and my stomach flip-flopped, like a fish caught on shore, gasping its last breath. Except in this case, there would definitely be a rediscovering of my supper unless I moved soon. I took a deep breath. That didn't help. I managed not to gag and opened my eyes more cautiously this time.

I think I liked it better when I didn't know where the smell came from.

I was in some kind of room. I imagined it was still the warehouse. For all I knew, this room was all the way across town, or another town entirely. But I didn't think I'd been out that long. And I remembered this smell when we'd entered the back of the warehouse.

I pushed myself up gently, my head protesting every single movement. Between the smell and the blow, I didn't think it would ever forgive me. I massaged my neck gently and squinted as I looked around.

Dead animals lined the floors. All types of dead animals. That was pretty much all I could tell from the various parts strewn about. Most of the corpses weren't actually in one piece. My stomach turned, realizing I sat on the haunch of something big. I shifted, tried not to think of it, forcing myself to analyze instead of emotionalize.

Damned easier said than done.

I liked animals. And a hell of a lot of them had been made to suffer here.

I spotted wild animal bits, like squirrels and rats. And some raccoons and skunks, which definitely didn't help the smell. There were also pets. Dogs and cats and even birds. Some collars flung about, covered in blood and fur.

I've never had a pet myself. But I liked the idea of one day having a pet, if guilds allowed that. And I imagined that this wasn't exactly how people wanted to find their furry friends. Maybe it was better that they never knew what had happened to their lost companions.

The heat of the warehouse intensified the putridness of the corpses, which baked slowly in the closed room.

I tried to blink away the webs of the injury from my eyes. Of the two lightbulbs hanging from the ceiling, one of them began to flicker slightly.

Great. Just great.

I touched the side of my face and rubbed away some of the blood. I'd apparently been using a swollen, half-ripped-apart raccoon as my pillow.

Wonderful.

I tried to ignore what I smelled like, looking around for Clay. The good part about being stuck with a bunch of ripped-apart animals was that it was easy to tell at a glance that there was nothing human amongst them. At least, nothing remotely big enough to be a Clay bit. Which meant Clay might still be alive.

But where was he? And why had I been thrown in here?

I carefully stood up, holding out my hands to steady myself. Dizziness washed over me, overtaking even the wave of stench surrounding me. I closed my eyes and focused on standing and breathing.

Eventually, the pain began to dissipate.

The room was maybe 25 by 25 feet, carpeted with a bunch of dead animals, no windows, and one door. One metal door, locked, I imagined. I'd grown up pretty much locked in a school or in a room. I was pretty good at getting past locks by now.

I took a couple of steps forward, fighting with my stomach, glad when it finally settled. The pain in my head receded from sharp stabbing to a dull throb.

A shower would feel so good. A bath. To change clothes. Remove every single layer of skin. My purple, probably rather black and blue at this moment, was also gore-covered. I walked carefully and slowly, trying not to trip on animal bits, or slip on the slick, bloodied floor. I didn't want more gore on me.

An eye looked at me from half a moose skull. I looked away, forced my stomach and head to settle again. The door was closer. But still so far. It was like walking in molasses, except all the molasses were in my brain and body.

A noise caught my attention to my left. A small whining. A dog sat there, or maybe a wolf. I wasn't exactly good at wildlife identification. It was grey and fluffy with deep black eyes. He'd been injured, a big gouge on the side of his snout. He looked underfed. His fur was matted, but he was alive.

"Well, there, Mister Pupper." I fell to one knee in front of him carefully, and patted his head. He looked at me intently, as though studying me.

"How did you get in here?" I asked. He cocked his head sideways. "Let's see if we can get out of here." I grinned at the puppy, patted him again and stood carefully back up, putting my hand against the wall as another wave of nausea and dizziness struck me.

Something touched my other hand, which dangled uselessly beside me. The dog had pushed his head into my hand, as though to comfort me. I smiled down at him. It was nice to have a friend.

Especially since my one other friend seemed to be missing. I pushed down my growing worry for Clay. I had to first make sure I'd live long enough to be able to find him.

The door wasn't even locked. I guess if all you were doing was keeping animal parts in here, it didn't matter. Then why was I still alive? Why would they just leave me here?

"Let's get out of here," I mumbled to my new friend as I carefully opened the door. The puppy bolted out but stopped to sniff the air. A low growl emerged from its throat.

I skirted the wall and tried to vanish into the shadows, but my head throbbed too much. I heard someone whistling and decided to head toward the sound. Not like I could avoid it anyway, so might as well face it head on.

The dog stayed two steps in front of me as though clearing the path. I turned the corner, the light from the fully lit hallway stabbing my brain. I swallowed hard. I needed water, my throat like sandpaper.

A man with a broom hummed at the music he listened to through his earphones. I stepped into the light, the dog beside me. It took him a few seconds for the man to notice us, and then he jumped back and pulled out his earphones, throwing his hands up.

"I'm just cleaning here, don't hurt me!"

"I'll consider not hurting you," I said with a gentle smile. Talking in this light felt like hammer blows. "But I need some information."

He nodded enthusiastically, as though he'd tell me anything just to make sure that he got out of this alive. I could see why, too. He was obviously no fighter. Or if he was, he was well-disguised.

He looked like a janitor, complete with a beer gut, cleaning products on his belt, a good broom at his side. And he didn't seem unhappy about any of that. The main thing that made him unhappy was me standing in front of him. I probably looked a sight. Bad enough a demon stood there. But a gore-covered demon? He probably wanted to take his spray and wipe some of that gore off of me. I'd be okay with that right now.

But first, questions.

"What is this place?" I asked.

"I.. I don't know!" he stammered. "I mean, I just get paid to clean the office areas! That's all I do."

"Are you a Traded?" I looked him up and down.

He shook his head. "No, you're actually the first one I've met. It's good to meet you, I think. You're not going to eat me, are you?" The words all tumbled into one another. A sweat mark began to seep through his overalls.

I felt bad for the guy, but not bad enough to back off. Still, I softened my voice a bit.

"Have you seen my friend Clay?" I gave him my most disarming smile.

More sweat appeared through his overalls. I probably had to work at my most disarming smile. I didn't seem to be having the desired effect.

"I don't think I know a guy named Clay. I mean, I think one guy in accounting's named Clay, but I don't know if it's your friend, Clay."

"I don't think he'd like accounting," I offered. We were practically making chitchat. That was friendly, right?

I looked down at the dog, who looked up at me as though shrugging and saying *this guy's useless*. I didn't disagree.

"Why are you keeping a bunch of dead animals back there?" I asked.

He looked wide-eyed toward the back.

"*That's* the smell. I kept...doesn't matter." He shook his head. "I'm paid to clean to the end of this corridor. I'm paid to keep the office area clean. And I'm paid to keep the main warehouse area clean—and I've got to tell you, there was a mess made in there last night..."

"Tell me about that." His eyes grew wide again. *Too enthusiastic, Tira.*

"I...I don't really know anything," he stammered. "I mean, there was some blood, and a few weapons strewn about. I mean, I think, if you ask me, I think they have an illegal fight club in there. But I'm not going to say anything, I just want to keep my job here, that's it! They pay well and I need the money!"

"No, I get that." I said, again going for friendly. Dealing with humans was more exhausting than I thought it would be.

"Who owns this place?" I redirected. The drumming in my head increased in cadence. I just wanted to shower and lie down. But I had no clue where to find Clay. I needed to learn all that I could. Even though I doubted the janitor knew much more.

"I don't really know that either."

"You don't know who your employer is?" My voice sounded crisp even to me. Definitely needed to practice being friendly more. I blamed my ringing head and the stench.

"I mean…" He looked flustered. "I'm not even paid by cheque. I'm paid under the table. But you're not going to say, are you? I mean, that way I can still afford everything by not having to… oh, this is bad, isn't it? This is bad," he looked even more distressed than he had when a demon had popped up in front of him. "You're going to tell on me, aren't you? Are you from the IRS?"

"The *what?*" I asked, looking puzzled. "What the hell's the IRS?"

"Um… okay. If you don't know that, that's okay." he said. Now he looked like he was about to faint.

I felt very much the same.

"Okay, well, I'm going to go away, I guess. So you can keep cleaning and stuff. Hey, do you know where my weapons are?" I asked with a smile. I could really use my weapons, in case I got attacked again. I probably should have clarified that I didn't intend to use them on him, since he grew even paler.

"Your weapons?" he asked, and he leaned against the wall. Oh shit. He was going to pass out, wasn't he? That wasn't great. Or he might puke. I was gross enough, I didn't need human puke on me on top of that. For all I knew, I had some on me already.

"Okay, never mind." I held out my hands in a gesture of peace. The dog whined. I agreed. "Tell you what, I'm just going to go, and you keep on cleaning, okay? Don't tell anybody that you saw me."

He nodded and leaned against the wall as I walked past him down the corridor. There were three different ways to go. I looked back. He pointed left.

"Thanks," I called out, my head now besieged by a steady hum. Time to go. The dog followed me and we soon found the main door and stepped outside.

The fresh air instantly cleared my lungs. I took a few greedy gulps followed by shaky breaths, the pain in my head clearing somewhat. The night was cool and crisp, and more like fall than early summer.

Perfection. Except for the aches, gore, and missing BFF, anyway.

"Stay close to me," I whispered to the dog, who didn't seem interested in going anywhere else.

I took another deep breath and closed my eyes, the bright security lights on the side of the building exasperating my head wound. After a few steadying breaths, I reached out to the shadows, and felt myself pulled into them, comforted by their embrace. I reached out and touched the dog, folding him into the shadows, too, so he didn't get scared by my sudden disappearance.

I walked carefully across the courtyard, intent on keeping us hidden and keeping us safe. I could head back to the halfway house. I didn't know where else to go, really. But there would be no Clay. And no one to watch my back.

I was all alone in a big, scary world.

In a strange and unexpected twist, I found myself missing the comfort and familiarity of my tiny cell in the school.

9

AFTER AN HOUR of traveling in cozily folded shadows, I felt pretty confident that we weren't being followed. I was also confident that I had no idea what to do next.

"Where the hell are you Clay?" I whispered. The dog beside me whined and placed his head under my hand again. I petted him. We kept walking together in silence.

"You don't have to follow me," I told the dog. I didn't think that dogs understood people, but some of them could be trained. I was pretty sure, anyway. "You can just head off and do whatever things you do. Dog things."

He ignored me and continued to be my silent shadow as we crossed into a slightly more populated area. I folded more shadows around us.

The strip ahead of me was covered in lights. Some

flashing, some steady, some colorful. People strolled about in amazing clothes, picking up the shine of the signs and reflecting it straight into my brain.

Usually I loved this area, but tonight, it made my head ache. My grasp on the shadows weakened as pain wrapped a vice around my brain. I leaned on a nearby wall and forced my feet to move down an alley. I collapsed beside a big garbage bin, having only natural shadows to rely on, the stink of the bin not nearly as bad as the one coming from me.

The puppy sat beside me. I wrapped my arms around my knees and lowered my head. Was it really only last night that I'd been in this same pose in solitary, when Clay had come to take some of the light away from me and keep me safe?

We'd been out here for not even a day, and I'd already lost him. I was in a strange world without a friend and without a destination. What was I supposed to do? Just pick a guild? How was I even supposed to do that? Pick up pamphlets?

Shit, I missed school. I'd hated it, but I hadn't had to worry about what to do next. Tears streamed down my face, and I let them, imagining they cleansed some of the gore from my cheeks.

No. I didn't miss school. I missed *Clay*. I missed not feeling alone in the world. And, truth be told, I missed having someone to guide me. I'd leaned on Clay for so long, following him into capers and battles, relying on his contacts and plans, that I didn't really know how to do any of it by myself.

That would have to change.

If I were to save Clay, I'd have to smarten up real fast.

"No weapons," I mumbled, the sound of my own voice snapping me back to the dark alley. "No friend." The dog whined beside me. I lifted my head, smiled, and patted him.

"One friend here. One missing friend." I corrected myself. The dog wagged his tail.

"First, shower and sleep. And food." It wasn't really a plan, but it was next steps. I could sleep the day away. Go back to the warehouse at dusk, when no one expected me and I wasn't in such rough shape. A good night's sleep would do wonders for me.

And I could look for tracks. Some kind of trail. Maybe my janitor friend would have stumbled on something.

I'd ask. Nicely.

"I guess we can keep each other safe," I told the dog as I stood up and stretched. Okay, time to stop moping and head back to the halfway house. I pulled up my hood over my head. I was a mess, but folding the shadows around me hurt my head too much right now.

I glanced at the street, surprised to see a few Traded walking with the humans. A woman with silver hair walked by, angel wings trailing behind her. Pearlescent skin, purple eyes.

An angel. She was an angel, just like I was a demon. I wondered again where the Traded came from, and where my true home was, knowing that the angel must wonder the same thing.

The sight of someone so different, like me, invigorated me.

"Let's do this," I mumbled. I put my hand on the dog's head, made sure my hood covered as much of my face as possible, stuffed my hands in my pockets, and walked out onto the crowded and fluorescent stretch of street.

No one stopped me. No one asked anything of me. No one even gasped at the sight of me.

Still, by the time I ducked down the side street and found the halfway house, I was exhausted. The day had taken its toll, not being able to hide in the shadows being the most taxing of all. I stumbled into the house and found our cots.

The room was still empty, so I collapsed on my bed, too tired to immediately bathe. Who cared, anyway. Everyone else, it seemed, had found somewhere better to be.

Now that I lay here, alone in the dark, I couldn't sleep, my mind riddled with worry. What had Clay told me before going on this heist? Not much of use.

But we had been tested the day before, apparently.

And Clay had acted a bit off when we'd left the school. I walked back through the day, reliving every moment and conversation.

Fatigue completely left me as I realized he'd deflected a very important question. He'd never answered if he'd received a guild invitation, asking me if I had, instead.

I hadn't.

I hadn't, and I'd told him.

But Clay had never answered the question.

I bolted up, ignoring the throbbing of my head, and turned on the small light just above Clay's bed. I looked at the sheets, the pillows, even under the mattress. I found nothing. But these hiding spots were all too obvious. If Clay had to hide something, he wouldn't have just left it there. Somebody would have stolen it.

What would he have done?

I turned to look at the dog, who sat beside the bed, looking at me with perked ears.

"Can you smell this, and figure out anywhere else that smells like this? Like, find the trail?" the dog cocked its head and looked at me. Let's go more practical instead of full sentences. I picked up Clay's pillow and handed it to the dog.

"Find him! Find where he went!"

The dog stood back up, sniffed the pillow, wagged its tail, and started to follow a trail down the room towards the back, where the door to the men's' bathroom stood. The dog wagged its tail at it.

I propped it open and glanced in. Nobody was there. I stepped in. This place was filthy disgusting. Not, like, dead animal room disgusting, but more like concentrated gross into one small space. The signs all over the walls that the Traded were responsible for cleaning their own space were ripped down or rebelliously filthy.

I tried not to look at what was on the walls and floors and ignore the wads of debris as I followed the dog.

I felt like I matched this place a bit too much. I really needed a shower. I needed a shower, and I needed a change of clothes, or at least to clean the ones I was wearing. And I needed to not be in this room anymore.

It wasn't the worst thing that I'd smelled over the last few hours—but it came close.

The dog led me to the garbage can in the back of the bathroom, near some urinals, which I tried very hard not to look at. He stopped, sat down, and stared at the garbage can.

"In there?" I asked.

He lifted his paw, as though to indicate it.

"Great."

Sometimes, it's best not to think about what you're touching, or what you're doing. I mean, I was wearing gloves, but even the gloves didn't quite feel like enough to block what I was touching.

Had I not been so suspicious of Clay's behavior, and wanting so badly to be proven wrong, I would have stopped. Hopefully I didn't find something really gross left there by Clay. Some bathroom habits were best not shared between friends.

I shuddered. This bathroom garbage was a great hiding spot, though. According to what I was finding, this hadn't been emptied in a long, long time.

I gagged a couple of times, my stomach rising into my throat, and pushed it back down, focused on finding whatever Clay had left there. Finally, I gave up on digging through the garbage and just kicked it over. This place was so messy that nobody would even notice.

A package covered in black cloth caught my attention. Clay wore exclusively black, so it could be his. Nothing else really jumped out at me, so I picked it up. The dog stood up, looking pleased.

"Good boy, Max," I said. Max. That was a good name for a dog. He was helping me, so he deserved a name, right?

Satisfied that I'd found what I needed, I walked out of the bathroom. The package could wait for now. I couldn't stand myself anymore, and I wasn't sure I was ready to uncover my friend's secrets just yet.

It was time for a shower. It was quite past time, really.

I stepped into the other facilities marked for women. A much cleaner space greeted me. I'd matched the other bathroom more.

Ugh, it was definitely time to shower.

"Come on," I told Max, and he followed along. I turned the shower on, pleased that it had hot water. I loved heat. I peeled off layers of clothes and threw them in the bottom of a shower stall, which looked refreshingly clean, and tossed some soap on them.

That could just get sprayed for a while.

I turned another shower on, already reveling the thought of warm water washing away the grime.

"Come on," I told Max, who also stank to high heaven. And that cut needed to be washed, so infection didn't set in.

He cocked his head, his ears on the alert.

"Don't tell me you don't like getting wet." He looked at me and took a hesitant step forward, then stopped.

"Come on," I stood up and coaxed him into the gentle stream. He went in, but looked really unhappy. He whined and wriggled a bit, but let me soap him up and clean him. I gently cleaned his wound, softly speaking to keep him calm as he trembled a bit.

Poor thing. Nobody should have to go through that.

Once I was satisfied with my work, I let him step out. He did and shook his fur dry, his tail low as he found a corner to sit in and lick off the remaining water.

"Everyone's a critic," I sighed, and then focused on washing my hair and skin, and then my clothing. The only thing that would have made this even more heavenly would have been a hot bath. I threw on my blue school jumper, which would do for pajamas, and hung my clothes to dry.

I felt drained. The heat had sapped my remaining strength and energy, but I couldn't sleep until I dealt with the black cloth, and what it contained.

"Come on, Max," I whispered. The dog stood up and followed, though he looked exhausted, too. I headed back to my cot. The whole place was still completely empty. Darkness still reigned outside, but dawn would probably break through soon.

Clay's cot felt more private than mine had, so I slipped into it instead. The dog lay down at the foot of the bed. I now understood what wet dog smelled like, but it smelled infinitely better than gory dog, so I liked it. I scratched his ear and he closed his eyes, snoring almost immediately.

I grinned, comforted by the presence, and took out the black bundle of cloth. I undid the knot and slipped the contents onto the bed. This was definitely Clay's. I recognized his scribbling on some of the papers. I guessed it was the details for our ill-fated heist. There was a name, a location, a time. That was it, but it was more than I'd known before.

I was surprised that Clay had written it down at all. But he'd been worried about his memory lately, having taken one too many hits to the head during all of his various fights. I guess he'd just started to cover himself to make sure that he didn't forget. That was smart.

Clay wasn't stupid. Lots of people thought he was because he didn't always speak his mind right away, and he tended to brood a lot. But he was sharp. He just didn't feel the need to announce his opinion every two seconds, like some people.

And Clay was loyal. Clay had never let me down before, and I certainly didn't intend to let him down either.

My heart dropped as I saw something else on the crumpled sheets. It was a medallion. Unless I was mistaken—and I knew I wasn't—it was a guild medallion. I didn't recognize it, but Clay had received an invitation to a guild. On one side of the medallion, some kind of explosion was depicted. On the other side, a mace—all spikes and strength and nastiness. Maybe he'd been invited to join some kind of demolitions club? I didn't know, and my mind grew foggy from pain, fatigue and worry.

Why hadn't he told me? Why wouldn't he tell me? Was it because I hadn't received an invitation myself? Was he worried about that? Maybe he'd hoped that he could bring me along, and just wanted to figure out how to first?

That had to be it. We'd never really been separated since we'd met at the Margrave Academy. And being separated now? Well, it wasn't the best feeling in the world.

"Be safe, Clay," I whispered, my words punctuated be the dog's snores. "I swear I'm going to find you."

The day had been long, and my head began to throb again. I turned off the light beside the bed, lowered my head, clutching the medallion in my hand, grateful that I wasn't alone with my dark thoughts.

10

A GROWL HUMMED in the background of my dream.

Clay and I are on a heist, running towards something and from something. It's dark, even too dark for my night vision, and I can't see him. I try to reach out to him, but he's nowhere. And I'm alone, unable to see anything, knowing I'm chased when I'm supposed to be the chaser.

The growl increased.

Followed by a bark. I snapped awake, my hand instinctively going towards the dagger that I normally kept under the pillow, sheathed, of course. I'd learned that lesson the hard way. Except the dagger wasn't there, and I remembered that I was weaponless.

The darkness over me changed in quality as a shadow crossed the threshold of my eyelids.

Before I could act, the dog barked, and his weight left the bed as he leapt. And then, a thunk and a yelp.

My eyes snapped open. I pushed myself to my knees —but before I could leap or get in any sort of position to attack, a blow came for the side of my head. I caught it with my arm, gritting my teeth not to yell with the pain.

Still on my knees, I managed to grab hold of the arm, so that the assailant couldn't strike right away. I punched towards the ribs, but he was too quick, shifting sideways. I quickly recovered and pushed myself off the other side of the bed. In one leap he cleared the small cot.

I ducked and brought up my arm, striking his chin. I backed into the empty space between rows of cots, trying to get to decent fighting ground.

I could see him a little bit more now, though he made it damn hard to be seen even with my night vision. Covered in black, with some jets of blue hair sticking out from the top, shorter than me and more wiry, he moved with the confidence of someone who expected to win.

That could work to my advantage.

His eyes narrowed—his eyes, which were completely dark blue without any white. They were stunning, and would be quite a distraction, if I hadn't been terrified for my life. And concerned about my dog, who hadn't made a noise since that thunk and yelp.

Anger ignited my limbs, and I gave up defending and went for a quick attack, faking left and bringing my knee up to hit him in the groin. He feigned, avoided my blow, but I grabbed his arm as he regained his balance and turned him back to put him in an arm lock.

Damn guy moved fast, shaking me loose as though I was a mere inconvenience, and threw me back against the wall. The impact jolted my entire body, stars erupting like a crazy kaleidoscope of glitter.

I slid to the floor, trying really hard not to lose consciousness. I doubted that would be to my advantage.

The back of my head smarted. My eyes stung with unspent tears. I pushed myself up to my knees, throwing my arms up defensively to brace for another blow. But it wasn't me he was after. He rifled through my things, pulled out Clay's guild sigil, pocketed it, and started to walk away.

Like hell!

I bounced up and was on his back in two bounds. I wrapped my right arm around his neck and held it with my left hand to choke him. He hadn't expected me to come at him again, so I managed to catch him unaware.

"Love your confidence," I said, wrapping my legs around him to force him down and knock him out.

"Get off me!" he answered in a gravelly voice. His

hand reached up, grabbed me by the back, and easily tossed me straight off of him.

Okay. Confidence wasn't great for either of us.

He was strong—a lot stronger than I was. I caught myself before I flew into the wall this time, hitting it with my feet instead, and used the force to springboard off the wall and back his way.

That would have been great, if I'd had a weapon on me. But I didn't.

Our eyes met, and for a split second, I could tell even in the dark blue eyes that he was surprised at my inability to just lay low when he obviously didn't want to hurt me, and just wanted me to go away while he stole what he needed to.

Showed he didn't know me—like hell I'd let him steal Clay's things.

In the split second this all happened, he pulled out a gun, ready to fire at my incoming head, looking discouraged. I managed to register that this was probably how I was going to die—alone, forgotten, body never found or identified.

If Clay still lived—and I hoped he did—he'd probably spend some time looking for me. But that was it.

Wow.

I brought up my arms to cover my head, instead of trying to pummel him. He fired the gun, the echoing sound followed by an angry yelp.

I hadn't gotten shot, but only because the dog had bitten down on his calf, throwing off the assailant's aim. I shifted right and landed an elbow on his nose.

He screamed, part in annoyance, part in pain, and I reached into his pocket and pulled the sigil out.

"That's mine!" I said, and jumped back.

"No it isn't, little girl," he responded. He definitely sounded annoyed. Maybe even a little bit more than annoyed. Definitely on the murderous end of things.

It was time to get out of here. I knew when I was outmatched. He was stronger and way better armed than me. I suddenly wished I'd have swiped a weapon instead of a useless medallion.

"How about we just call it a day?" I said, putting my hands up. Maybe I could talk my way out of this one. "I mean, you're not going to get this without a hell of a fight. And, as you can see, I can give a hell of a fight." I grinned my most disarming grin. "So maybe we should just call this even, as it were? And just go on our merry ways? What do you think?"

His right eyebrow rose very, very slowly. The only reason I could see his eyebrow was because I'd shifted his face covering when I'd thwacked him so hard. That made me feel doubly good.

"Give me the medallion," he said, "and then you can walk away. I've no use for you."

"Well, that's nice," I answered, "but it's my friend's medallion, and I'd like to give it back to him. So how about you just leave, and once I find my friend again and give it to him, we can maybe have a talk, all three of us, and see if you should get it. Does that sound fair?"

The dog came around and stood in front of me, ready to pounce. I felt better for having an ally. As good as my negotiation techniques were, I didn't think I was winning this one.

Laughter erupted from the assailant's lips. It wasn't immediately clear to me whether that was good or bad.

"I'm almost sorry that sigil isn't for you!" he said. "I think you'd be fun to have around! But no. It's not. So you either give it to me, or I'm going to have to kill you."

Negotiations were definitely not going well, I decided.

I did a quick scan of my surroundings. There were no windows for me to escape out of, and the door was much too far for me to make it.

Two daggers flew into his hands. He lazily twirled them around, obviously comfortable with throwing them.

I *could* give him the sigil. But it was my only clue to finding Clay. I wouldn't just be giving up this piece of metal. I'd be giving up Clay.

And I wasn't ready to do that.

"No," the word slipped from my lips before I could think better of it.

Three actions happened in quick succession. None of them were mine, because I just stood frozen in surprise at my own answer. My survival instincts were not super refined, it turned out.

The first thing that happened was that a knife went flying from the right hand of the assailant—a smooth, easy, almost lazy arc straight towards my chest.

The second thing that happened was that the dog threw himself in its direction and howled in pain.

But he kept his forward thrust, as though the knife formed but an inconvenience, and went straight for the assailant's throat.

The third thing: Max hit his target, and dark blood shot out.

The assailant screamed and backhanded the dog into the wall. Max crumpled and didn't get back up.

The assailant clutched his throat. I didn't think it was an arterial bleed. It wasn't gushing strongly enough for that. But he was thrown off balance.

I leapt forward, kneed him in the gut, and managed to steal one of his daggers as I swept past him.

He grunted and fell down, blood still dripping from his neck. And then, gentle smoke rose around him - wisps of purple clouds hugging him, not unlike a gentle lover's caress.

He vanished.

"That's a neat trick," I said, my hand going to the

back of my head where it had hit the wall. It came away covered in blood.

I'd live.

Max!

He panted, but his eyes were wide and still conscious, his tongue lolling out of his mouth. The knife had hit his shoulder. With any luck, the wound would heal and not grow infected.

"I'm going to have to pull this out," I said. Max stopped panting for a second as though he understood. I placed my hand over the wound, then pulled the knife out quickly. He yelped but didn't bite me. I covered the wound as best I could, not exactly sure how to do first aid on a dog.

"Let's get out of here," I said. I grabbed my bag and Clay's few things. I picked up the dog. He was heavy so I wouldn't be able to make it too far, but he couldn't walk in his condition. And I wasn't the type to leave my friends behind—especially those who'd taken a knife for me.

We stepped past the still-empty desk, out of the dark and soul crushing space of the halfway house, and into the night.

Shadows have always brought me comfort, but I couldn't help but stare into them with suspicion. Had that fighter been alone? Which other Traded would come here, and what could they do?

I needed to find somewhere safe, and I needed to do

it quickly. Max's breaths were a bit too quick and uneven. He needed to rest and heal.

I folded the shadows around us and walked down the alley as quickly and quietly as I could.

"Shhh," I told Max, afraid he'd whine. But he remained quiet, despite his erratic breathing. There had to be some kind of apartment or some abandoned place where I could find refuge. Somewhere where people wouldn't expect me to be.

I still had a few hours before dawn, and tomorrow was Sunday. If school hadn't lied, which they might have, it should be a quieter day tomorrow, which was good. Might buy us more hiding time in one place.

I turned down the busy strip, which was much quieter now, though a few people still wandered around. I barely had the time to register what people wore or what they were doing, focusing on keeping the shadows wrapped around us, holding Max, being quiet, and finding someplace safe to sleep.

That was a big to-do list, as my head ached and buzzed with fatigue now that the adrenaline had left my body. The strip grew quieter the further I walked. After a few more blocks, I spotted a furniture store, its lights mostly dimmed.

Within, I could see its setup, all fake walls creating display rooms. I walked by its door, and glanced at the store hours. They wouldn't be open again until noon tomorrow.

I grinned. The walls would hide us from the street, and we would be safe for a few hours. We could sleep, heal, and be gone before the workers came for the day. And no one would look for us in a fancy store.

Perfection.

"Let's go rest," I whispered to Max.

I headed to the back of the store, found the door.

"I'm just putting you down a second," I told Max, who looked at me with big woeful puppy eyes and panted as I laid him on the pavement. I dropped my shadows, so he wouldn't lose sight of me and panic.

This furniture store didn't take the chance of theft seriously enough, as far as I was concerned. I easily picked the lock and disarmed the alarm system within a minute.

"Come on," I told Max, and gently picked him up. He gave a tiny whine. "I'm sorry," I said. "We'll be comfy soon."

He remained quiet and I slipped in, locking the door behind me.

"I think we'll be safe here," I told Max. I found a nice bedroom layout in the back of the store. Great setup, and secure from the outside view. The lights in the back of the store were turned off, only a few lights lit near the front.

I gently put Max down at the end of the large, plump bed.

"Let me see your wound," I said, and he lowered his

head as though bracing for the blow. It wasn't bleeding anymore, which surprised me a bit. "You heal quickly," I said. "Good boy." I patted his head and his tail wagged a bit.

Relieved that he would be fine, I slipped into the bed. I still wore my blue jumpsuit, which was a mess now, covered in blood and dog fur. Too tired to care, I snuggled in the sheets, the dog a comforting weight at my feet.

I wondered who our assailant had been. The way he'd spoken, it sounded like he was from the same guild that had invited Clay. I wish I'd have asked more questions, but I hadn't really had the time with him trying to kill Max and I.

Why had he come to collect the medallion? How had they known it would be there?

I stared at the dark ceiling, Max's snores comforting my dark thoughts. They knew, because they had Clay, and they'd made him tell them. I imagined them torturing Clay, and I gripped the sheets tightly in my fists.

I now deeply regretted not having killed the assailant.

11

I DON'T RECALL EVER HAVING BEEN on such a comfortable bed. The mattress was squishy, the sheets wonderfully soft, the duvet (a duvet!) poufy.

Not that I had much experience in the matter, but I was pretty certain that this was, in fact, the perfect bed.

I snuggled deeper into the blankets, trying to come up with a plan, still coming up empty. If I could have followed the man, I might have found Clay. I had no idea what to do and, to make matters worse, I'd have to get up soon. The quality of the light was changing, so dawn was breaking.

Not ready to commit to the day, I focused on the sounds around me and the comfort of this bed. The ticking of a clock somewhere deeper into the store. The buzzing of the front window lights left on overnight, to ward off the darkness. The slight snoring of the puppy at my feet.

I frowned. That didn't sound quite right. The quality of the snoring was a bit long and deep for Max. And had he taken up this much room on the bed last night?

Alerted that something was off, I suddenly became very, very awake. I'd hidden the dagger underneath the pillow, grateful I'd had the presence of mind to do at least that much.

I found the hilt and took comfort in it. I shifted gently. The breathing and shape were all wrong for Max. What had they done with him, and why were they sleeping at my feet?

Creeptastic.

The form moved slightly and stopped snoring.

They were awake, too.

Time to move.

Fearing the blanket might entangle me, I didn't bother trying to stand and just sat up, ready to stab. I half expected to find a well-armored and well-armed assailant at the edge of my bed. Instead, there lay a curled-up, very naked man.

I hesitated. I hadn't exactly expected this.

The man's eyes flew open and grew wide as he saw me staring at him. He threw himself off the bed, landing with a thud.

"Who the hell are you?" I demanded, pushing the

blankets off of me, putting some distance between me and the naked man.

"I'll just go!" he said. "It's okay!" he added, as though to comfort me.

"I'm not the one who's going to need comforting!" I spat out. "Tell me who you are and where my dog is, or I'm going to eviscerate you!"

He didn't immediately answer, and I didn't feel like waiting him out.

"Come up now or I *will* kill you."

Two hands popped up, followed by a head and a naked torso. He remained kneeling, so that's as far as I saw. Which was fine by me. This day had been shocking enough already, and it was just beginning.

"Look, if you'll just let me leave," he repeated, "I'm sure that you'll find your dog again..."

"I'm sure that I'll find my dog again," I calmly interrupted, "when you tell me what you did with him. Possibly while I'm eviscerating you."

He sighed in frustration and looked sideways, towards the front of the store and the infiltrating dawn.

"I can't get the puppy," he said, "unless you let me go."

"We'll see about that." I shrugged, flipped the knife, caught it by the blade, and extended my arm back to throw it at him. I aimed for the shoulder, but I was still pretty sleepy and willing to hit his face instead.

"Wait!" he shouted. "Look carefully into my eyes," he added, sounding rather grumpy.

"I'm not gazing into your eyes," I offered, extending my arm again. "This isn't some kind of romantic encounter, despite the fact that you were in bed with me."

"It's not," he sputtered with even more frustration. "Look, *I'm* the dog, okay?"

Well, that made me pause. I didn't lower my hand though. I squinted at him and stared into his eyes. They were dark, just like Max's, yes, and they definitely weren't human now that I looked more closely. Their central darkness spread out too widely. He didn't blink quite enough, either.

"You're a dog?" Disbelief dripped into my voice.

"I *can* be," he offered. He ran his hand through his wild, brown hair.

I looked more closely at him now—at the way he moved, at his body. He was muscular but lean—not wide, like Clay. Smaller, more agile. Stubble lined his jaw. His movements seemed measured, but not in the way a fighter's were. More like an animal deciding whether or not to bolt.

In the end, it was his eyes that convinced me. Dark, steady, unwavering. Like Max's.

"Max?" I asked.

"My name is Ian."

"That's not a good name for a dog!" I retorted.

"I… no, I guess it's not?" He looked both confused and even grumpier.

"Max is a good name for a dog," I said.

"My name is Ian," he repeated, ignoring everything I'd said. Maybe I'd just call him Max when he returned to his puppy form. He looked less grumpy as a dog.

"Wait, can you go back to being a dog?"

He shrugged. "I can. I can be a dog, or any other animal, depending on my mood and how I shift my energies."

"Oh," I said, now lowering my arm. "So you're a Traded?"

"I am. Like you."

"Why didn't you tell me before?"

"Well, I was a dog…" he offered, sounding a little bit less grumpy. But still pretty grumpy.

"Well, that makes sense, I suppose. Couldn't you just change back?"

He shrugged. "If I could control my powers, things would be a little bit different. But I can't fully. It doesn't matter. Can I get up now?"

"Sure," I said. "Do you have some pants?"

He blushed slightly. I grabbed a bathrobe from the side table, throwing it at him, the tag still hanging off of it. It was pink.

Very pink, in fact. And very fluffy.

He slipped it on, looking suddenly more

comfortable, less naked, and a hell of a lot more annoyed.

I grinned and sat on the edge of the bed. "So, what's your story? Which school did you go to?" Not that I knew that many schools. They'd been pretty strict about keeping us separated by school and maybe a tad unaware. I supposed they didn't want us organizing or knowing exactly how many of us there really were.

"Not all of us ended up in schools," Ian said, standing up. He was pretty tall. He hesitated but sat down on the end of the bed. He still looked ready to bolt.

"Oh, I thought we all did." Then again, why would the school have supplied us with that information? I shifted my focus to the more immediate. "Why were you in that room with the dead animals?"

"I don't quite remember," he said. He looked down, his gaze flickering again from grumpy to annoyed, followed by puzzled. He seemed to shrug it off and looked back at me. "But you want to find your friend."

"Oh," I said, "so you understand even when you're a dog?"

"Mostly," he replied. "I have a lot of animal instincts and different ways of looking at the world, but yeah, I'm still me."

"I took a shower with you," I said, and he turned bright red.

"I didn't…you insisted on cleaning me!" he stuttered.

I bust out laughing. It felt damn good.

"You did stink quite a bit! So why would you help me find my friend, though?" I paused, debating whether to trust him or not. So far, trusting Max had worked out. "So, what's your story?"

He looked annoyed again. "What story? I mean, I've mostly spent my life living in the bush, taking animal form as often as I can to avoid people, because people are terrible."

I couldn't disagree with that one.

He calmed down, his voice suddenly more muted. "And you helped me. You got me out of that room, where all those other animals were dead. I assumed that was going to be my fate too, so I owe you."

"You don't owe me anything," I said, turning sideways to look at the vanity, now that I was confident enough I wasn't about to be attacked by the strange man. "Besides, you took a knife for me, so we're even."

I started fixing my hair in the mirror. I looked a mess. I needed another shower. I pulled out my clothes, which didn't look much better than I did. Sticking them in my bag while still wet and not pulling them out to dry hadn't been my best move.

I needed new clothes, and I needed more weapons. So many more weapons. Maybe there was a clothing shop around here that I could raid. And a weapons shop. Did those two things come combined? That would be pretty sweet.

"I *do* owe you, though," Ian insisted. "You saved me and showed kindness to me. That's my code."

"That's nice," I said, "but your code has nothing to do with me. Look, we had some fun, and I enjoyed your company, but I don't need someone in a pink robe trailing after me. I'll go find Clay by myself. You do you. I don't want you getting killed on my account. That was close enough last night."

When he didn't answer, I stopped fixing my hair and turned to look at him. He seemed fixated on the floor, but his gaze was far away.

"Hello?" I said.

"Look," he focused back on me. "Like you said, I don't know how I ended up in that room. And I don't know if whoever put me there will be coming after me again. And you don't know whether the people who are trying to get the sigil will come after you, either. So, I'm just thinking that maybe we're stronger together."

I looked at his shoulder.

"Is your shoulder healed?" I asked.

He nodded. "I heal when I shift form. It's one of the benefits of becoming human again. A limited benefit, though. Then I have to have conversations with people." He practically growled that last part. I couldn't help but laugh.

He looked surprised.

"Alright," I relented. "You're right, I could probably use the help. I have no idea what I'm doing, and if you've been out here longer than me, then you know more than I do. So let's start with finding Clay. Do you know where I might find him?"

"I think I recognize the sigil," he spoke slowly, as though measuring his words. "I think it's from one of the fighter's leagues, and I think they're dangerous. It might be wiser to not confront them in person."

"A fighter's league?"

"Yeah. You know, one where they pit Traded one against the other."

"Oh," I said, "like a gladiator thing?"

He shrugged. "Look, how badly do you want to find your friend?"

"Clay's my only friend," my voice cracked, suddenly choked up by a distressing amount of emotion. "We've been hanging out together, protecting one another, doing heists together, and always making sure that we both made it back. I can't just let him go now. I can't just decide that he's probably okay, that he's joined a league. That he hasn't been kidnapped and isn't about to be murdered. I can't do that. He's my friend, Ian. I have to go after him."

He seemed surprised by my impassioned plea. He wasn't the only one. I don't think I'd stopped to really consider the ramifications of losing Clay. But now that

I was out here alone with a pink-bathrobe-wearing stranger as my only friend, I needed one thread to my past. That thread was Clay.

My foster family didn't care for me. Nobody at the school liked me. I hadn't received a guild invitation, so I wasn't even sure what would happen to me in a couple of weeks. Clay might know. Clay always seemed to have an idea, or a contact, or a mission to go on. Clay intended to make sure we stayed together, and no one else would do that for me.

I needed him in my life. I *wanted* him in my life.

"I need my friend," I told Ian. "I won't just leave him behind."

"That's fair enough," Ian said softly. He seemed to consider the problem, his hand absent-mindedly holding the soft pink robe closed. "I know one place where a lot of Traded go. And a lot of the guilds recruit people there."

"Don't they just recruit people in the schools?" I asked.

"You really know nothing of the world, do you?" He looked at me with wonder.

I shrugged. "I've been at the Margrave Academy for thirteen years. So, no. I know what they told me, which doesn't seem super complete. Clay knew more, and he knew people outside the school."

Ian looked at me steadily. "Clay was the only one with contacts?"

"Yes." I shrugged again. "I never needed to have them. *He* had them."

Ian studied me for a few more moments. I grew uncomfortable under the scrutiny, remembering that I looked like a purple demon, afraid he'd just clued in that he might need more normal friends. Or at least wiser friends.

When he did speak, his soft voice reassured me. There was no mockery in it. "No, not everybody ends up in schools. A lot of the Traded were already recruited before your cohort was let loose into the world. The rest are just being sought out by the guilds now."

"We have two weeks to *choose* a guild if we don't have an invitation," I said, "that's what they said."

"That's what they *told* you," he said, not unkindly, "but it was a lie. You don't really get to choose. The guilds choose you. You don't get to decide how you're going to be useful. *They* decide. Whatever skills you've developed, whatever you've proven apt at, that's what they're going to use. And you're useful at several things. They're going to come for you."

He hesitated, pondered his words, and then continued, as though thinking about something else.

"Really, they're probably already here." The resignation in his voice made the hairs on the back of my neck stand on end.

"Time to go," I said. "Lead me to this place, and let's see if we can't find out where Clay might be."

"Alright," he sounded a little bit more like his grumpy self again.

"Do you want me to find you some clothes?" I asked with a grin.

"No, it's fine." He ran his hand through his hair. "Just remember to be safe." He said, fixing me with his unwavering gaze. And then he turned, and his body began to crumple, folding in on itself, much like I folded the shadows around me when I vanished. I couldn't see well over the pink bathrobe, but within moments, Ian was gone, and the dog was there instead.

"Right," I said. "Time to go." I pulled the pink bathrobe off of Ian's furry back.

"You know what? I think I'll still call you Max in your puppy form. It's a much better dog name." The dog looked grumpy, but didn't bite, so I grinned.

"Let me get ready and we can go," I said, then cocked my head. "Are you going to stay here while I get naked again?"

He quickly turned and vanished around the corner.

I grinned, glad that Max/Ian was still with me. Until I found Clay, it was nice to know that I wasn't completely alone in this world.

I HATED BEING out in the daylight. I'd avoided it like the plague before going to school and, once there, the only time I'd ever left the school was at night time, when Clay and I snuck out.

But there was definitely no waiting for darkness today. We couldn't exactly hide in the furniture store, as tempting as it was. Some of those chairs looked amazingly comfortable, but the store owner might take offense to us just sitting there utilizing his fine wares, while his customers tried to shop around the strange demon girl and her dog.

We'd left enough of a mess, too. I'd made the bed, which hid the messy sheets, but the duvet cover had been very white before this. I hoped the scribbled apology note would make them feel a bit better. In retrospect, I probably shouldn't have used some of their for-sale stationery to leave it.

Oh well. Live and learn and all that good stuff.

I followed Max down the street. It was hard to imagine he could turn human, even though I'd just seen it.

He sniffed the ground once in a while, and I could tell he kept an eye out. Which was great, because that meant I could keep my hood over my head. I could try to fold the shadows around me, but the sun beat down and my shadows might fail or prove insufficient. I might remain inconspicuous with my hood up. I definitely wouldn't were I half a mirage or if I just popped up randomly.

I kept my face down so that hopefully nobody would see the purple tone of my skin. I had wrapped a towel around my neck, like a scarf. Thank goodness for the chilly morning and decent store stock.

Oh. I probably should have mentioned the towel in my apology note.

I focused on following Max. I didn't need to look up for that. Thankfully the streets weren't too busy, but they were still busy enough to make me feel ridiculously exposed.

My hands were deep in my coat pocket, my fingers wrapped around the guild invitation that Clay had ignored. Is that why he'd gotten in trouble? Because he'd ignored them, and they'd come for him? Or had he gotten in trouble because he was trying to do something for them, and maybe he'd hoped that I could prove myself and be invited to join the same guild?

Had we failed the test together, or had he passed and I'd failed? Should I have let the little girl die? Maybe. I didn't think I wanted to belong to a guild that was okay with that, though. And neither would Clay.

The edges of the sigil felt hard on my skin, as though it wanted to cut my skin, leave scars, mark me as its property forever. I wondered if that's how Clay had felt when he'd found it on his bed. Or when he learned that I hadn't received an invitation.

Or maybe he'd been worried that we'd been summoned to two different guilds, and that we'd be separated. Maybe he'd even been relieved when I hadn't received an invitation, and thought that he could perhaps drag me to his guild instead, where we could continue to just hang out, be friends, ignore the world as much as we could.

The world didn't want us in it, anyways. The past day had only made that amply more clear to me.

I turned down another street, following Max on the sidewalk. He was definitely more of a Max than an Ian, at least when he was in dog form. I hadn't paid attention at all to where we were going, lost in my own thoughts and worries.

I glanced up carefully. The streets weren't quiet, but the quality of them had changed. There were people milling about, but few people showed their faces, all cowled like I was.

Tall buildings lined the narrow street like silent stone guardians, keeping out the sun. No beam even reflected off a glass surface or window, as though the street was meant to be kept dark at all times, no matter what.

I found myself relaxing at that thought.

The sidewalk vanished, and we walked directly on the pavement. That hardly seemed to be a problem, because there were no cars here. I felt comforted by the shadows and slipped into them a little bit more. Not enough to completely vanish, since Max was a bit too far ahead. But enough that anyone looking at me would see a figure passing by, her face hidden in more shadows than they'd expect from that cowl and scarf alone.

A trick of the light, they'd surely think.

I walked with more confidence, the shadows like a gentle hug.

Max suddenly stiffened, stopped, sniffed the air, and turned to look at me. I met his gaze, and in them now I could see not just the big round eyes of a dog, but also the intelligence of a man. It was obvious once you knew to look for it.

Which I hadn't before this morning.

He looked significantly at me.

"I don't know what you want from me," I sighed,

holding out my hand. "You're a dog. If you want to tell me something, you're going to have to like, change or something."

His ears and his tail lowered, and I wanted to apologize, but I also wanted to ruff the fuzz around his face.

"Alright, I'll follow," I said. He perked up one ear and cocked his head. "And, I'll be careful," I added. That seemed to satisfy him and he continued leading me, although more slowly this time. I paid more attention to my surroundings.

"Don't walk so quickly," I whispered, knowing that he could hear me with his canine ears. "Stay close to me so that I can keep you in the shadows as well."

His head cocked a bit, as though considering what I'd said, and he slowed down. I wrapped the shadows around him a little bit. He could still be seen, but couldn't be spotted as easily.

He was like me, more of a mirage than a presence.

We turned down another road, which proved even darker than the last. There were quite a few people here now. I stopped for a second and Max did as well, sensing my hesitation.

These people...they were all Traded. It felt like being back in school, except not at all, because we weren't all wearing the same uniform. We weren't all lining up in a row, hoping to avoid a thrashing. Instead, these were all just Traded, standing together, laughing, chatting, walking, some drinking, some eating.

Living their lives like normal people.

I'd never seen anything like it. I honestly never thought I would.

I found my feet again and walked forward slowly. Max stuck close to me.

There were carts with goods for sale. I went by a row of them, far enough from the vendors not to be spotted, but close enough to see strange meats and foods that smelled delicious. Some of the carts sold weapons, all shiny or black, and deadly looking.

I liked those ones best, but I didn't have any money, and I wasn't sure how wise it would be to try to swipe something. I imagined not too wise.

A few carts had clothing, and some sold ridiculous shoes. I loved them all! And I loved the people walking the streets even more. It was way better than the main strip in town. This, this *Traded* street, was the most amazing place I'd ever been!

Skin tones came in every color of the rainbow, even purple like me! Some folk had one head, some had two heads, some had no heads! Limbs came in multiple counts. Some had feathers, some had fur. Most looked human enough, but some didn't look human at all. There was this giant thing that looked more like an enormous June bug than a person. I wanted to say hello and hear their voice, but Max led me away from them.

Most amazing of all, there was a lot more laughing than frowning. And there were a lot of people hugging as well. Some were holding hands.

Is this was the Traded could be like?

I stopped and leaned my back against a nearby building, just wanting to take it all in, afraid I'd walk into something if I kept gawking and going forward. Max sat near me, glancing up at me with a knowing look.

I had heard rumors of areas where the Traded gathered. I assumed they were dark seedy bars, with angry looking folk itching for a fight or a drink to forget their troubles. Not a community or a lifestyle, but a place to hide. But here? Here was different. The Traded were walking around, not hiding their features or what made them *different*.

As though this was their *community*. As though they belonged. My mind and heart reeled at the thought of those things. Two things I'd never expected to find outside of Clay.

Some of the Traded held guild sigils proudly, pinned to their uniforms or their clothing. Others showed no sign of belonging to anything. Like they only belonged to this moment on this street in the shadows of buildings that had been built long ago, before we even existed on this world.

Two men walked by, hand-in-hand, laughing. They didn't glance my way. I realized that I'd pulled the shadows around me and Max. Trying to process the unfamiliar and unexpected sight, I'd slipped back into what made me feel most safe.

I looked down to Max and he seemed to nod, as though telling me: *It's okay. You can let your defenses down, for just a moment. It might not hinder, and it might even help.*

Three laughing friends walked by, each eating something that looked like a mix between ice cream and pudding. It looked amazingly delicious. Clay would probably enjoy it. And, for all I knew, Clay might be around here, too. Or somebody might know where he was, or what the sigil meant.

This was why Max had brought me here. He'd brought me here so that I could find the information I needed to find my friend. But I couldn't do it from the shadows. I couldn't do it hiding here. And maybe, just maybe, this light would be willing to look me in the face, and I could find friends here, instead of those who feared me.

I took a deep breath and counted to ten.

Then I lowered my hood and I stepped out of the shadows.

13

Stepping out of the shadows wasn't nearly as dramatic as I thought it would be. I dropped the protective fold and nobody seemed to care about the purple-skinned demon girl. I took a deep breath and lowered my hood.

Nobody paid me anymore mind than before. I fit in. Nobody seemed to even notice me!

And that was all well and good, sure, but how was I supposed to get information on Clay? I mean, who the hell was I supposed to talk to about anything? And how was I going to broach it?

"Hey, how's it going? Have you seen my sort of blood-thirsty, thuggish-looking friend? Do you know about this particular guild that might have gotten him kidnapped and potentially killed?"

I looked down at Max, who glanced back up at me. He seemed to be about as out of ideas as I was. *Great.*

Another recluse who wasn't good at speaking with people. I really needed Clay. He was decent at talking to people. He could certainly always get the information we needed.

A few people walked around us. They didn't glance at us suspiciously, or like we didn't belong here

Despite that, I still felt so...*seen.* And I wasn't necessarily a fan, still.

"What do we do now?" I whispered to Max. He wagged his tail and looked at some nearby Traded.

"I don't know what to ask, Max," his tail stopped wagging. I stood frozen in place, unable to do anything but feel *noticeable.*

My fingers were still wrapped around the sharp edges of the sigil. I needed to know about this guild. I needed someone to tell me where it was from. I just wasn't sure how to go about that without attracting all sorts of negative attention.

Was I overthinking it? I mean, these were still people, just going about their lives. Some of them had probably gone to school like me. Others had grown up in the bush like Ian. But we were all Traded, so we had each other's backs.

Right?

Really, I just needed to talk to one of them. If I just talked to one of them, then hopefully I could get the information I wanted, or at least be pointed in the right direction.

I was suddenly struck with inspiration. If I could get one of them to tell me where people shared information, where somebody had their fingers on the area's pulse, and especially that of the guilds, then I could probably find the path to Clay.

So I wasn't asking random people about the guild, or Clay. I was only asking who I could get information from. Excitement coursed through my veins as I worked through the idea. I was looking for a guild to join, after all. It made sense that I'd ask around about who knew about the guilds!

Confident enough in my theory, I took a deep breath, twisted my lips into what I hoped was a charming and welcoming smile, and took a step forward.

And then stopped dead as Blake stepped in front of me.

"Hey demon girl!" he said, his lazy grin promising only pain and ridicule. "Stepping out of the shadows? Does it feel good, being out in the light?" He stood uncomfortably close to me. I could smell his breath. It was even more annoying that it smelled good, like peppermint.

The upside of meeting Blake, however, was that Blake knew Clay. Chances of Blake wanting to help me weren't exactly high, but maybe I could get something out of him.

"Have you seen Clay?" I asked, trying not to let my

disgust show on my face. My lips twitched, trying to maintain their smile. I was pretty sure it was slipping steadily away from disarming.

He snorted. My fingers curled into a fist, but I kept my hands in my pockets. Two of Blake's buddies from schools stepped up beside him. I'd never bothered to learn their names, just referring to them as Blake's shadows. It seemed to still fit, and I wondered if they'd all been sent to the same guild.

Of course they would have been. Guys like Blake had all the luck.

"D'you lose your buddy?" he asked in a teasing tone. Had he adopted a British accent? Pretty sure he had. Did he think it gave him some kind of air of authority? Probably. Blake was such a loser. I needed to talk to someone else. He wasn't worth spending sanity points on.

"Never mind," I said. "I hope you're having fun out here, in whatever guild actually decided to put up with you."

I tried to walk away, but he stepped in my way. Max growled. Blake snorted.

"I see you've found another reject for a friend? Maybe you don't even need Clay anymore."

Out of sheer reflex, my knee came up, intending to connect with his groin and leave him on the ground. But before I felt that satisfying crunch, my knee stopped all forward momentum, frozen in the air, disappointingly short of hurting Blake. I stood there on one leg, not able to go further with my knee, and not able to bring it down, either. I glanced up at him, surprised. He leaned in further.

"If I were you," he said, uncomfortably close, "I would just forget about your buddy, and go find yourself a guild that will put up with you. Probably one of the circus guilds would love to have a demon to show up, don't you think? I mean, look at you. You don't even fit in here, where it's all Traded."

He shot Max a warning glance, who now stood between us, baring his teeth.

"Losers," Blake whispered, in his definitely new British accent, a smirk on his lips and a dangerous glimmer in his eyes. Then the pressure released my knee and I could move my hands again. I let my foot fall, but didn't back away from him. I knew better than to back away from bullies and give them any ground.

I also knew that my chances of landing a blow on him were non-existent, so I just glared at him.

"Bye, Tira," he drawled, now sounding a tad more southern, apparently still refining his new accent. He turned his back and walked away, making it clear he didn't see me as a threat. His two shadows gave me a look that I think was meant to be threatening. I glanced back at them, and they moved a little bit faster, closer to Blake.

Max nuzzled my hand and I gently patted him.

Blake was wrong about so much. Clay was worth too much to give up on, and I certainly never would. Blake had been right about a lot, too, though. And that stung. I still didn't fit in here. I didn't know how to approach anyone. I still only hung out with outcasts, and probably would never do anything *but* that. And I still didn't know where Clay was. But if one good thing had come out of meeting him, it was that I now understood a little bit more about Blake's powers. He'd stopped my movement, because he'd seen me coming.

I vowed that if ever I were to confront Blake again, I'd make sure that he didn't see me coming. He wouldn't have the chance to stop me twice.

"Let's go," I told Max. He began walking towards the right and I followed him. I had to trust that Max had my best interests at heart. I had to trust that someone in this world still found it worthwhile to lend me a hand.

14

____

I WONDERED if Max led me somewhere to get information, or simply led me away from Blake. I was okay with following either way.

The crowd thickened around us and I resisted the urge to merge back into the shadows. I focused on Max, finding it difficult to look up and meet eyes. I pulled my hood back up, deciding it was a worthy compromise to not folding in the shadows.

People parted to let me walk through, either out of suspicion or kindness. A few tried to pet Max, but he growled at them. A small smile graced my lips. It looked like I wasn't the only one who was done with people today.

I followed my grumpy buddy, analyzing people's boots around me. Or feet, if there were no boots. There was a lot of good fashion. The Traded seemed to excel at good footwear. There were tall boots and short ones, heels and no heels, there were fancy runners with shiny laces and holographic covers, there were some studs and some zippers, some leather and some synthetic.

The feet without shoes made me glance up a few times. Hoofs leading up to a perfectly normal looking person. Twigs to branches with sentient movement. Hovering feet to crystal wings and elongated bodies.

I looked down at my own practical black boots and thought that I needed to go shoe-shopping. And that, should my feet be free, they'd just look purple. But I didn't have hooves, like some of the people here.

Weren't demons supposed to have hooves?

The quality of noise and amount of feet around me changed and I looked up.

This area didn't seem as old. They were a few newer builds, made of some metal I couldn't even recognize. The metal seemed to absorb the sunlight instead of reflecting it, so it still felt comfortably shadowy down here. There were fewer Traded, too, and I found myself breathing a bit more easily.

Crowds were a problem, regardless of race or origin.

I glanced inside one of the nearby shops. It wasn't a shoe shop, much to my disappointment. Maybe a soap shop? Were soap shops a thing? The individual working inside was also a Traded, her eyes a little too wide to be human, her skin a little bit too blue. But something else struck me. She seemed older. She looked to be at least forty.

But the Traded had all arrived here twenty years ago, as babies.

I stopped and glanced in, then slowly kept walking when Max nudged me with his nose.

"Is that person older?" I asked Max. He looked at me, and then looked at the person in the window. I swear his little doggie eyebrows lowered, perplexed.

In the distance, at the end of this street, I spotted an older woman with white hair and a stooped posture. She looked like a grandmother, except that wings protruded from her back. Great, leathery wings, which she'd accessorized with delicate pink tulle to soften them.

It certainly worked. Nobody seemed terrified of her. But she did seem like a grandmother to me, as she vanished into one of the stores. That was really strange. There shouldn't be any Traded old enough to be grandparents. We were all new, weren't we?

But then, we probably all aged differently. It made sense. Different races from different worlds. I tried to imagine that, aging faster than anyone else around you, and I was suddenly grateful to age at the right speed. Or at human speed, I guess.

I did enjoy the pink tulle idea, though. Maybe dressing all in black was too scary and didn't help my demon-ness. I looked good in black, but maybe I should try more sparkle and flair?

I shuddered at the thought of standing out on purpose. *Scratch that idea.*

Max sniffed the ground a lot, which caught my attention. Maybe he'd managed to get Clay's scent. He'd found that emblem in a dirty gross bathroom garbage, after all, so his sense of smell wasn't in question.

My heartbeat quickened and my focus sharpened. Max began walking faster, still sniffing the ground. I accidentally shouldered a few people as I went by, and didn't care.

Clay. He was nearby. He had to be, or Max wouldn't be moving this quickly, this enthusiastically. He'd been so cautious so far, but now he seemed possessed to move at a greater speed. He brought us down a smaller side street, blessedly empty of people.

Max stopped abruptly just before the corner and I almost ran into him. He looked back at me. I nodded and folded the shadows around both of us.

I peeked around the corner. It was a darker alley, but not dark in the way that human alleys were. Dark in the way that a Traded might make it.

I reached down and crouched, holding Max in my arms to make sure that he was fully hidden from view.

I didn't know how useful my powers could be against a Traded who could fold darkness like that. Was it similar to my own powers? And what did they want to keep hidden this badly?

It was probably a guild entrance, I realized, my pulse quickening. I'd never actually been to a guild. We'd had open houses at the school, sure, but those were all tables lined around the gymnasium with smiling humans telling us what was so awesome about them, giving us the impression that we'd get a choice.

If what Ian said was true, that had never even been in the cards.

I crouched down near him, quiet, holding on to the shadows. I looked down the alley, focusing my eyesight beyond the darkness. The closer I pulled the shadows to me, the more I could pierce the darkness ahead. I realized that I was pulling the shadows from the alley, gathering them around me.

That was strange. Did I always move the shadows when I manipulated them?

I almost yelped in surprise when two burly-looking individuals walked right by us, not spotting us. I'd been so intent on the darkness ahead that I hadn't been paying attention. Neither had Max, from his jump.

The two men carried a limp form between them, feet dragging on the ground, head dangling, long hair falling wildly around it.

I couldn't see much of him, but I could see the shape

of his body, I could see the width of his arms, I could see the details of the clothing just enough to suspect that they dragged Clay. My heart skipped a beat and my hand went for the dagger in my boot.

As though sensing what I'd seen, Max stiffened and focused his gaze back on me. I looked at him, wishing I could communicate with him, not daring to even breathe a word. The darkness of the alley had rallied again to cover the two men, and the pull called on my shadows, too. Keeping them wrapped around us proved challenging.

I have to save him, I wanted to tell Max. But something stayed me. I don't know if it was Max's large eyes, staring back at me with worry, or if it was that power, pushing back against my own.

Or maybe it was the fact that Clay seemed unconscious, but alive. And the knowledge that even if I found a way to beat those two surly looking guys, who were probably Traded, I'd have to find a way to drag Clay out of here. I was strong, sure, but Clay was heavy. I couldn't help him if I got captured, too.

I hated myself in that moment. I hated my lack of courage to step out of those shadows and take my chances, to grab my friend and run.

I clung more tightly to Max, who seemed to relax at the assurance that I wasn't about to desert him. We crouched silently and focused on Clay. I forced my eyes to pierce the darkness, to watch them drag him into one of the two thick doors in the alley.

And then I waited, breathing deeply, for those dark shadows, deeper than my own, to dissipate, so that I could follow.

15

I MISSED my weapons even more ferociously than I had earlier. I had one dagger and one throwing knife (thanks to the assailant at the safe house), and that was it.

The weight of the shadows around me seemed to vanish, turning into just my usual comforting cloak. I released a long breath and shared a look with Max.

"Time to go in," I said, giving him a confident grin. Clay would have been convinced. Now so with Ian. Or so I gathered from his growl.

"Look, the weird darkness is gone. I can sneak in, folding shadows around me, find him, wait 'til he's awake, and then we can both walk out of there. It's a perfect plan!"

I didn't need to be able to understand him to know that he wasn't buying what I was selling.

"Well, I'm going to help my friend," I stood up. "You stay here like a good boy."

He half-growled, half-snorted, and his fur began to recede, revealing human-looking flesh. His paws turned to hands and feet. He stood up beside me.

"You're naked again," I offered.

"Keep your eyes up!" he growled at me.

"No problem," I said. "But I'm going after Clay."

"I know." He sounded genuinely distressed. "I just think that there might be a smarter way to do it than just walk in there, don't you?"

"Sure," I offered, "I'm sure there are multiple smarter ways to do this. I don't have another way right now, so why don't you come up with something?"

"I can sneak in there and at least see where your friend is. Then I can report back and lead you directly to him, instead of having you wandering around in there."

"I can hide in the shadows," I cocked an eyebrow. "Besides, I think people might be suspicious of a dog walking around."

"I can be more than just a dog," Ian offered. He didn't look like a Max at all right now. "Look, let me go in there and figure out who exactly they are and what they're doing, and where they're holding him. He's unconscious right now anyways. What are you going to do, drag him out of there?"

I shrugged, crossed my arms. "I can probably wake him up."

"I'm sure you can," he looked discouraged. "But he might be loud about it. Can you wait while I go in and investigate? Will you trust me with that?" He sounded more and more exasperated.

Worse: he made a good point.

"I don't know that I have that much of a choice," I mumbled.

"I'll take that as a high compliment that you trust me then," he sarcastically noted.

I ignored his tone. "How long are you going to take?"

"Give me half an hour," he said. "I can get in there, scout around, and come tell you where he is."

Half an hour seemed like forever right now. Half an hour was enough to do a lot, including kill Clay. But if they'd wanted to kill him, they would have surely done so beforehand, and not bothered to drag him into whatever this place was.

"Can you do it faster than that?" I asked, my tail twitching. I hated when I lost control of my tail, like some unruly accessory. I forced it to stop moving, kept my eyes up, staring into Ian's eyes. He seemed to consider the question.

"I guess it depends on how big the place is..." he pondered. "I'll come back as quickly as I can, half an hour *tops*."

"I guess that'll do." He raised an eyebrow at me. I gave a short laugh. "I appreciate it. I really do. Thank you, Ian."

He seemed a bit less grumpy as he nodded and began to shift and change. His body mass shrank down but I kept looking up, not really wanting to see how his body collapsed in on itself. I waited a few more seconds, since I knew this didn't take very long, and when I looked down, a little mouse looked up at me with those strange, dark eyes.

I crouched down and offered my hand. The mouse jumped in and I brought it up closer to my face. It was super adorable, with big ears and eyes. Were mice good pets? They must be, with so much cuteness in such a tiny package.

"So you're a mouse now?" I said. The mouse squeaked.

"You still kind of look like a Max," I said. Little annoyed mouse faces are even cuter, it turned out. "Half an hour. That's all I can give you."

The mouse held my gaze for a second longer, then it scampered off and wiggled its way under the door.

I stood folded in the shadows, waiting for any sign that he was in trouble. Laughter from the nearby street pierced my concentration, and I allowed myself to breathe. I didn't have Clay yet, no, but I knew where he was.

He was alive.

And Ian would find him.

Which would take about half an hour. There wasn't much I could do here. Maybe, just maybe, I could get a tiny bit better equipped for this endeavor. I grinned, glanced at the door one more time, and then slipped back toward the alley and the merchants, toward the passers-by who were busy with their conversations, toward the merrymakers and shoppers.

I headed back toward all the Traded who were not necessarily keeping an eye on what they carried. Folded deep into the shadows, I went to see what weapons luck would let me borrow this day.

16

Within twenty minutes, I was back at my spot outside of the door, better equipped with two more knives, one gun with two bullets (thanks for loading up, buddy), one cheese grater—which could make an awesome weapon in the right circumstances—and also one shiny blue, very high-heeled shoe.

I wondered what had happened to the other shoe, pondering if I had somehow destroyed some fairy tale moment by taking the lone shoe. That thought amused me and I grinned.

This wasn't exactly my best grab of weapons, but it wasn't too bad, either. And there wasn't any time to be picky

Twenty-two minutes. Ian had eight more minutes before I headed in there. I tried to focus and stay calm, taking deep breaths and thinking about the present moment. The blood flowing in my veins, the earth under my feet, the strength of my limbs…but I couldn't help but think about Clay. How could I focus on anything else but my friend who was in there—hurt, unconscious, beaten.

I would hurt people. My hand twitched in anticipation.

Clay needed me, and I was out here with a high-heeled shoe and a cheese grater. Somebody would feel that damn cheese grater on their face.

Movement caught my eye, and the little mouse reappeared, making its way towards me. Relief washed over me as I knelt down and put out my hand, wrapping the mouse in my shadows so that Ian could see me. The little mouse hopped in and I raised him to eye height.

"I guess you're not changing," I said.

The mouse cocked its head as though indicating that he couldn't. Maybe he could only change so many times in an hour. I had no idea how it worked. I really had to ask him more questions next time he was human.

It would help if he was clothed, maybe.

"You and I are going to have a talk once this is over," I mumbled. "For now, lead on, tiny buddy."

I lowered my hand and he hopped off, heading back

under the door. I followed and waited a few moments, hearing the latch give. I opened the door, the mouse dangling from the pin pad beside it, chewed wires sticking out.

I picked up Ian and brought him close to my face again. "Don't get electrocuted," I whispered. He gave a quick squee and I put him down, following him as he scampered across the room.

I don't know what I'd expected, but this wasn't it. Plush carpet covered the floors. Wingback chairs were grouped to host conversations in each of the four corners. Bookshelves filled with old paperback volumes lined the walls.

I thought I'd be walking into some kind of warehouse district, or a cold metal corridor. This was none of those things. I almost felt bad walking on the carpet with my boots.

I could see the trail of Ian as he made his way through the lush carpet. I followed, grasping at the shadows as I walked forward. There was an odd quality about the shadows here, and I realized that I couldn't quite figure out the location of the light source. There were no windows, so it certainly wasn't from that, but neither were there lamps, or lightbulbs, or any type of visible lighting mechanism. It was as though light just seemed to exist because it needed to. And that light made the shadows difficult to grasp.

I couldn't hide in them as deeply as I wanted to. I

still felt exposed as I moved quickly across the room and out of it, into a grand entryway. A staircase made of marble led up to a secondary level, the higher floor lined with a beautiful detailed walkway across the entire perimeter. That same strange light emanated from everywhere and nowhere at once.

A rare shiver travelled up my spine. There was something off about this place, in the way the light and shadows danced.

Ian kept moving forward, not attuned to the shadows like me. His little body scampered near the ground, all sorts of adorable. I followed him quietly, crouching low.

Ian didn't go up the large staircase, rounding it instead. Behind the staircase stood an archway, covered in marble. Without a door it seemed inviting, except for the fact that it hid behind the giant staircase.

I crept in, surprised that it led to a sterile-looking room. Every inch of the room, from ceiling to floors to walls, was covered in impeccably clean stainless steel. And that was it. Nothing else graced the room. No piece of furniture or decoration to speak of.

The only comfort I found here was the obvious light source from two old fluorescent lights wedged in the ceiling.

Ian kept going, crossing the room to another set of stairs leading down. He hopped from one stair to the other in a remarkably quick scamper (also: adorable).

Whatever strange light had lit the first two rooms gave up here, as did the strange shadows. This darkness felt comfortable and known. I wondered if mice could see in the dark, and decided they must, because Ian still moved ahead pretty quickly. So fast that I was losing sight of him.

I sped up, not wanting to call out to him and draw attention to us. Just because we hadn't seen anyone, it hardly meant that no one was within earshot.

I wrapped the shadows around me tightly as I descended, feeling better for their comfort, like slipping into a favorite sweater. The air changed in quality, to cooler and more damp. The metal stairs gave way to concrete ones.

I much preferred heat.

I'd lost sight of Ian, but there was really only one way to go, and that was down. After what felt like hours, I reached a concrete floor. I looked back, and saw no one following, or any indication that anyone would. I listened ahead, and couldn't hear anything. No even Ian, but his little mice feet were pretty quiet.

I took a step forward, then stopped. Something didn't feel right, but I couldn't tell quite what. I glanced at the stone walls, and the concrete floor. It was completely dark here, but I could still see fine.

Maybe it was just nerves from being down here alone. This place was pretty creepy. It reminded me of the academy's basement, and I had bad memories of that place.

I looked back the way I'd come. The shadows seemed undisturbed. I tried to shake myself free of growing anxiety. Just bad memories mixed in with fatigue and worry. I pulled the shadows more closely towards me as I took another couple of steps forward.

And that's when I realized what had been bothering me. It was the quality of the shadows. They were different. They were like the shadows that had been in the alley—like somebody else manipulated them and made them their own. Not in the way that I did, but on a much bigger, scarier scale.

"Welcome to my home, Ms. Misu."

I whipped around at the voice, but before I could act, a stifling cloud gripped my brain. The shadows turned against me, whipping away from me and exposing me. I grabbed the shoe and threw it where the voice had come from, thrilled to hear a curse as the shoe connected.

The shadows moved around me and blocked everything else from sight. I couldn't pierce them, no matter how hard I tried. I hesitated, but decided to call them, to see if some would hide me. The shadows had never denied me before.

Nor did they this time. They came to me as soon as I reached out to them, and folded around me. For a moment, I felt safe within them. Then, something lifted me up in the air, knocking the breath of me.

The shadows were crushing me!

I pushed back against them, willing them to leave me be, but they obeyed a power greater than my own. A power intent on destroying me.

17

When I was six years old, my foster dad came into my bedroom, and I learned that I could fold the shadows around me. To him, I was gone. Vanished in the blink of an eye, nowhere to be seen.

I hadn't realized I'd done that. I just didn't want to get hurt.

I took a deep breath, stifling a cry, and he struck where the sound came from. He connected. The next day, I turned seven, and I was sent off to the Margrave Academy, without a goodbye, just loaded up in a bus full of other kids like me.

Except they weren't like me. They looked human, unlike me. And they mocked me.

I didn't belong, even with those who were different.

I would never belong.

Wrapped in layers of sadness in that bus, the shadows didn't wrap around me, though they whispered comfort at the edge of my mind.

Three weeks later, fighting lessons began, and nobody wanted to spar with the demon girl. Nobody but Clay, who made me feel like I could belong.

He was good. He loved fighting. We learned together. I grew more confident. Within a few months, I was getting good at avoiding blows.

Clay was getting great at giving them. And he gave one too many, some kids deciding to teach him a lesson one night.

Word travelled fast in the school. Always had. By the time I found them all, Clay was half dead, dragged outside the school where they could easily beat him. I caught them by surprise, threw a couple of our latest toy—smoke bombs—grabbed Clay and started to run.

But he was hurt and I couldn't drag him all the way to safety.

"Leave me," he insisted, his face bloodied under the full moon. I put him down near a tree, hid in its shadow.

"I won't," I insisted.

We were seven. We were scared.

And the bullies, also seven, came.

You learn fast when you're terrified.

"Go," he insisted, spitting up blood. I shook my

head, hell, my entire body. I wouldn't leave him, but I was terrified and didn't know what to do. How would I save my friend.

My only friend.

"I won't leave," I whispered as they approached, calling for us, not having spotted us there. Clay passed out. I held him, closed my eyes, willed us safe.

Just like I had in my bedroom.

And they passed us by.

The shadows danced around me, keeping me safe. It took me years to learn to work them, and fold someone else in them.

But they'd always provided safety.

Until now.

The shadows wrapped around me tightly, holding me suspended.

I couldn't breathe. I couldn't scream. I couldn't fight back.

So I closed my eyes. I was that little girl in a schoolyard again, under a full moon, in the shade of a tree, cradling her wounded friend, wanting nothing more than to save him. I was that girl again because I'd never stopped being her, and I was even more scared now, and my friend needed me.

The shadows loosened and gently put me down on the ground, folding carefully around me, as though apologizing for their betrayal.

But their care wasn't enough as something struck me hard in the side, sending me flying into the wall.

"This could have been so much easier," the voice said as the shadows engulfed me.

THE SHADOWS WHISPERED TO ME, beckoning me back to consciousness. Or maybe that was just the sound of my body being dragged across the floor. Yup. That was definitely me being dragged, my head swooshing back and forth, making me a bit nauseous. My arms were somewhere over my head, my feet up where someone held my ankles and pulled.

I didn't open my eyes yet, not quite remembering how to anymore.

That had been a good hit.

It took me a second longer to realize that my side really hurt. Not a little pain of "maybe I shouldn't have tried to jump out of that window without first checking if it was open and landed on my ass," but a feeling of "wow, someone really hit me in my ribs and I caught that blow full-on, and now I'm regretting my life choices."

I paid attention to my breath as they continued to drag me. It came out easily enough. I didn't think ribs had been broken, which was lovely.

After going through that string of realizations, I started to debate what I would do. Somebody was pulling me, or two people maybe. Hard to tell, as my eyes were still closed. I didn't know if I still had any weapon, but I imagined that I didn't.

I was a little bit sad about losing that shoe, though. I'd looked forward to seeing what else I could do with it. Not to mention the cheese grater!

My hands seemed untied, which was great, but also could be a sign that they didn't see me as a threat. That was less great.

Just when I'd decided that it was time to open my eyes to gauge where I was, who was dragging me, how many were in the room with me, and whether I could escape, the movement stopped, and my feet dropped.

Unless I was mistaken, not that much time had passed. That was a little bit comforting, but not that comforting. I wanted nothing more than to drag the shadows back to me and vanish within them, but that particular comfort was no longer available to me.

I sighed and opened my eyes. Nobody was in my immediate field of vision. To be fair, my immediate field of vision was the ceiling. But it was still nice to know that no one was hovering over me.

I decided to risk sitting up, although my ribs throbbed and complained.

"We didn't think you'd be joining us this soon," a gravelly voice said, the same one from the corridor. I focused on it, Well, I tried to focus on it, anyway, slightly distracted by the room, which looked like a throne room. It was ornate enough to be one.

The walls were that same surgical steel, intricate etchings on the cool surface, light emanating from them. In its center jutted a raised platform, right before me. On it stood what seemed to be a captain's chair from one of those sci-fi shows, with some medieval stylings thrown in for flair.

I forgot about my hurting ribs as I examined it. I *loved* flair. It was big, complex, detailed, and the man who had just spoken sat lazily on it, comfortable with his rank and position. Whatever those might be.

Several others stood by, obviously Traded. One had orange eyes, another four arms, yet another green skin. All of them were wearing black and armed to the teeth. They all looked very threatening and ready to step in between me and the man who I could only assume to be their boss. Maybe even king. I mean, he *did* have a throne.

I spotted my cheese grater hanging off the belt of the green-skinned woman and narrowed my eyes at her. She grinned my way. Attacking her for a cheese grater didn't seem like my best idea. Neither did attacking anyone here, really. It struck me how many different looking Traded I'd encountered since leaving school, and yet I still always felt like I didn't belong.

I'd have to think on that more later, when I wasn't about to potentially be skewered.

I focused back on the man. I imagined he was a Traded, but that was equally impossible to tell. There were no immediate markings on him to showcase him as such, but if so many mean-looking Traded seemed afraid of him, or at least willing to worship and protect him, he had to be one, right?

I guess? This world was damn confusing.

He was tall, wide-shouldered, with an athlete's body. Warm eyes set in his dark face. No hair on his head. But he didn't need any to hold the attention of everyone. He was dressed fully in black, which seemed to be the party color here.

I could make out no sigil or guild emblem on any of them. I tested my side and slowly stood, holding my hands away from my body as a gesture of peace.

"Hello," I said. "This is nice," I indicated the chair with my chin.

"Indeed it is," the man said, seeming more amused than annoyed. I hoped, anyway.

"What business brings you here today?" he asked after a moment's silence. I debated lying, but doubted that would get me far. Anyway, I knew from vast, *vast* experience, that I was a terrible liar.

"You're holding one of my friends here," I lowered my arms to let them rest beside me. "I saw you drag him in. I was wondering if I could have him back please. We had plans."

"Oh, you had plans?" the man said, raising an eyebrow.

"We did," I shrugged. "So, can I have him back?"

"Your friend," the man's amusement seemed to fade, "stole something of value. We're trying to see if he's willing to tell us where he took it, so that we can obtain it."

"Oh," I said, "did he realize it was of value to you? Because sometimes information isn't very clear, so it might not be his fault. But I'm sure that he'd love to help you regain it, if it was something of yours to begin with."

I hoped I was better at hiding skepticism than I was at lying. Clay didn't care. Clay just wanted to get the job done, get the money, and get out. But Clay didn't want to die, either. These people with all of their various weapons and grimaces looked like they wouldn't mind killing a Traded that wouldn't be missed by anyone.

By anyone except me.

"You'd think he'd be willing to just hand it back to us?" The man looked extremely skeptical. Couldn't really blame him for that.

"Well, I mean, if it means that much to you…"

"Tell me, Ms. Misu," he said, surprising me that he knew my name, and then I recalled that he'd said it right before I'd gotten attacked by the shadows. Had he been the one controlling them? How did he know so much about me? This whole situation just kept getting less and less comfortable.

"Do you think that your friend would retrieve the item to save you?"

Well, now I was *definitely* uncomfortable. I shrugged.

"Probably. But," I added quickly, "if your well-armed guards aren't willing to go retrieve it from wherever he brought it, then I'm guessing that he might need some help. So how about you let him and I take care of that, and bring it back to you?"

For a few moments, his features didn't move at all, and then one of his eyebrows rose ever so slowly.

"You think we'd trust you enough to just let you go?"

I smiled. "Well, you seem to know my name, and I'm guessing that's not the only thing you know about me." He didn't deny it. Even less comforting. "You tell me, do *you* think you can trust us to retrieve the item?"

He didn't answer for quite some time. I was trying to think of something witty or convincing to say, but words failed me (not too surprisingly). I looked around nonchalantly to spot some kind of escape route, or a way to get armed. Neither seemed highly likely.

The stench of damp reached my nostrils. This throne room stank. That removed some of the sheen from it.

The man kept glaring at me, studying me (aka creeping), and finally spoke. "We'll just have to see, won't we?"

Any follow-up questions I might have had were cut short when he indicated for two of the guards to come and take me.

"Thank you for your time!" I shouted back as they shepherded me outside of the throne room. I hoped Clay would be smart about this. I had no idea what he'd stolen, but these people wanted it back. From the knife now pointed at the base of my back, keeping me very alert, and very, very worried, I somehow felt that it was imperative that I convince Clay to cooperate with them.

Clay could be stubborn, but he was also loyal.

This building hadn't seemed that big from the outside, but from within it seemed endless. We crossed three corridors, the shadows slipping around me, just out of my grasp. Two more guards joined the two escorting me.

Seemed like a bit of overkill. It's not like I could slip away into the shadows—they'd already proven that. And it's not like I had anywhere better to be, really.

We entered a corridor with cells lining each side, thick bars barring any escape. Very dungeon-like. Medieval stuff was pretty cool, but maybe more so when not about to hold you captive. They opened the door to one small cell and pushed me inside. I wanted to swear at them and demand my cheese grater back, but instead stared open-mouthed at the inside of the cell.

Right in front of me, looking as surprised as I did, stood a very beat-up and bruised Clay. We closed the gap between us and wrapped our arms around each other.

We were trapped. We were in trouble. We might soon be dead. But hell, at least we were together.

19

CLAY and I had never really been huggers, so it got awkward pretty quickly.

"I'm so glad to see you," I said as soon as we broke apart.

He looked perplexed.

"What are you doing here, Tira?"

I laughed. "I came to save you, of course!"

"I don't…I mean, thank you, but, Tira, these people, they're not good."

He looked genuinely worried.

"I know that," I said. "That's why I'm here to help you, you big doofus!"

His eyes lowered, the right one so bruised it could barely open. I wish I'd stolen an ice pack instead of a cheese grater.

"I think I really screwed this one up," he said softly.

He looked back up, as though having resolved to look me in the eye. "Look, uh, I just...I didn't want to tell you, but..."

I pulled out the sigil from my pocket.

"Yeah..." He didn't look surprised that I'd found it. We'd been friends a long time, and knew each other's beats. "That."

There was no bed in his cell, only four walls and some bars. He sat down on the floor. I joined him, leaning against the wall.

"Which guild is it for?" I asked. I didn't speak loudly, but my voice seemed to echo down the corridor. I guess we wouldn't get much privacy here, even though I couldn't immediately see any guard outside.

"Not sure of the name yet," he answered, giving me a slight grin, which only highlighted his split lip, "but I know it's a fighter's guild. One of those leagues you hear about all the time. Like MMA fighters, except all Traded. Going in the arena and just fighting it out, and winning, and getting the prizes, and the glory, and..." he paused, as though surprised by his own outpouring. He shrugged. "I guess I was just interested in joining, you know?"

"Why didn't you just tell me that you'd received an invitation?" I said, hating the hurt that slipped into my words.

"Well, I wouldn't have left you behind," he immediately said. "I mean, that's why I asked you to come with me on the heist. I figured if we proved ourselves in this first real test, then you could join too, or maybe they had a friend, buddy pass or something. I don't know how these things work yet. But, when you didn't receive an invitation to a guild yourself, I figured this was the perfect chance to show them what you're made of. You're tough, you can take a good fight."

I gave a bitter laugh. It didn't feel tough lately. "I couldn't even fight someone off with a cheese grater," I said bitterly.

Clay thankfully didn't ask for elaboration.

"We're just having a bit of a down time," he said, trying to pump us up. "You know, leaving the school, and out in the big wide world, we don't really know anyone or anything...so I think we've just got to give ourselves a bit of a break here, and prove what we can do."

"Prove what we can do to whom? The ones in this guild?" I asked, looking around the cell walls.

"No, not these ones," he said. "These guys, they're more dangerous. But I like the fighter's league. That's the kind of stuff you want to be in, you know? It's not a circus league, so you're not stuck wearing some weird makeup or doing some weird shit on stage for people's entertainment. You get to beat people up, and you still get some of the glory and the accolades, without having to make a fool out of yourself."

"But you'd get your ass handed to you in front of everyone," I countered.

"I wouldn't," he grinned with a knowing smile.

"Oh?" I said. "Looks like you got your ass handed to you, Clay."

"Not by the fighters league, though. By these mean sons of bitches here."

"Well, these mean SOBs are the ones who have you," I said. "Were they the ones who found us in the warehouse? What the hell were we after there, anyways?"

"Oh," Clay shrugged the question aside. "No, these people here, they're a lot more dangerous."

"What do you mean? What do you know about this place?" I asked.

"Not a whole lot. Except I know that the fighter's league is afraid of them."

"So they sent you to retrieve an item to show your loyalty to them? Or because they were too cowardly to take it on themselves?" My blood began to boil.

Clay knew that look and put a calming hand on my arm.

"I'm not sure, to be honest. As far as I can tell, we stole the item from a third guild, another fighter's guild, maybe. These guys here," he nodded at the cell, "just happened to want the item we got to first. Then there's the league we're auditioning for. So, three guilds. One canister. And we're caught in the middle.

I'm not sure why. But I have no doubt that you and I can figure this out together."

"I don't disagree about that," I said. "except that we have no weapons and no leverage. They're going to ask you to get whatever you stole back from the fighter's league."

"I figured they might," Clay said, leaning back against the wall and closing his eyes. "Might as well rest up then. Get ready for the battle."

"That's not a bad idea," I said, looking at his wounds. He healed quickly, but I wasn't sure he could heal quickly enough to be safe in battle again by tomorrow.

"You're so hurt, Clay." Sorrow accented every syllable.

"I'll be fine," he kept his eyes closed.

"I know," I said softly, and then added, "you know, they're going to kill me if you don't do this, right?"

Clay's eyes shot open again and focused on me.

"They said that?" he sputtered.

I nodded.

"I won't let them," his voice gained strength and left no room for argument.

The way he uttered those words made me believe him. He always found a way to make me believe him. Something in his confidence, his sheer willingness to tackle any problem, his refusal to admit that he might fail. And Clay rarely did fail. There were temporary setbacks, sure.

But we succeeded, always. Together.

"We'll handle it together," I said, and grinned at him. "Hey, who knows? Maybe I *will* get to join that fighter's league too, and we'll get to hang out there."

He nodded, as though pleased I'd finally caught on.

"You will," he said. "It's going to be a good time, you mark my word."

"Sure, except we're about to steal your entry exam back from them."

He shrugged. "That won't screw us over," his eyes widened, his lip curled up, "I mean, as long as they don't *realize* it's us, anyway."

I laughed, the sound echoing down the corridor. He leaned his head back against the wall and closed his eyes, pleased that I was on board.

And I was, too. We just had to be smart. And quick. And not be seen.

Which might be a hell of a tall order if the shadows didn't prove more cooperative the next time I called them to me.

20

After an hour of silent resting, two guards came and motioned for me to follow them. Clay opened his eyes and nodded to me.

"I'll see you soon," he said. I nodded back, feeling less confident than he did, and followed them.

They brought me down two corridors. I was starting to get a fairly solid map of this place, which provided me with some comfort. That knowledge could be useful, should an opportunity to use it present itself.

We passed from the sterile corridor to a stone one, and then back to stainless steel. This building had either been extended, or built very strangely. I spotted a few Traded, all dressed in black and looking like they had someplace to be.

This place could use better décor and more cheer.

The upstairs was so pretty. Why was it so dank down here? And why didn't they do more fun stuff up there? I guess hauling prisoners around wasn't much fun. Plus, upstairs had lovely windows. Not the best when undertaking shady activities.

The guards unlocked a door and motioned for me to go in, backing away so as not to give me the chance to attack. I stepped into the room, the door closing behind me.

Two deadbolts loudly clanked into place. But this wasn't a cell like Clay's. This seemed more like a guest room, with a small bed, and even a sink to freshen up. Sure, there were no windows, the bed was bolted down and the door was locked, but this place felt absolutely heavenly compared to Clay's cell.

I'd barely reached the bed when the door behind me opened again. I turned around, and in walked Ian—not in dog form, nor in mouse form—in human form. And for something different, he actually wore clothes—the same dark clothing that everybody else here seemed to be wearing.

He looked remarkably uncomfortable, for someone who wasn't naked for the first time in front of me.

"I'm so sorry you got caught," he sounded genuinely sorry.

"Are you with them?" I asked.

He nodded. Then furrowed his brow. "Mostly, anyway. But I didn't realize this was one of their outposts. That was a surprise to me, too. I wouldn't have brought you in here like that if I'd have known."

"Can you get me out?"

He shook his head.

"Can you get Clay out?"

He shook his head more vehemently. "No, your friend pissed them off good. There's nothing I can do for him right now."

"What did he take?" I asked. "What's in the container?"

He shrugged. "I'm not even sure. But I know it's important to Sonsil."

"Oh. Is that the boss on the throne?"

Another nod. "He's not to be trifled with."

"I got that." I paused. "Are they going to kill me? And Clay?"

"Not if I can help it," Ian said. His voice softened with something different than discomfort or grumpiness.

"At least I know that Clay's fine for now," I said with a grin. "Maybe I'll be able to join his league, too, if I pull this off."

"That doesn't matter right now," the harshness in his voice took me by surprise. "What matters is that you manage to get back alive. This isn't a game, Tira!"

"Well, what am I supposed to do?" I asked, frustrated this time. "All that I want to do is make sure Clay's safe, make sure I'm safe, and find somewhere for us to be. We only have two weeks, you know, after we leave school. You don't know that, because you didn't go to one of the schools," I said, and then I immediately regretted my words. His face betrayed no emotion, but I felt like I'd attacked him regardless. He'd done nothing to deserve it.

"I'm sorry," I said. "I'm just feeling jittery. This has all been very annoying, and they took my cheese grater. I like my cheese grater, Ian. I was going to do something with it. Don't know what…probably grate a face."

"You had a cheese grater?"

I shrugged. "Yeah, I stole it from the cheese merchant. Why would a cheese merchant have a cheese grater? Don't you think they'd just, like, sell blocks of cheese?"

Ian shook his head. "You're difficult to follow sometimes, Tira. But listen, be careful. Stay safe. Don't trust anyone."

I looked up at him. "Are you telling me that I shouldn't trust you?"

He stiffened a bit at that, and then seemed to reflect on it.

"I guess that's up to you to decide," he said.

"I guess it is."

"Just… just be careful." He sounded exasperated. "I'm not sure that you can fully trust Clay, either."

I narrowed my eyes and stared at him. "Don't

question my friend. We've been through thick and thin together, for a long time. I know who I can trust."

He held up his hands before him.

"He's your friend, I get that. But I'm not sure he's telling you everything you need to know. And I think he wants to be part of that fighter's league badly enough that he might put you on the line to get in."

"Clay wouldn't do that," I said softly, too tired to spit it out. "You don't know him like I do."

"Alright," Ian offered. "This isn't my battle to fight anyways. Just please be careful."

"You've said that like five times," I said. "I can't do anything else but go forward and help Clay, Ian. I *won't* do anything else but that."

I couldn't start to question Clay now. We'd been friends for so long. I trusted him, and he trusted me. That still had to count for something out here, even when we weren't at the school. If best friends couldn't have each other's backs, then what was the point of it all?

"I'll see you later," Ian said. "Just be care—"

I cut him off. "I know. I know."

He looked like he wanted to say something else, but didn't quite know how, so he just walked out. The door closed behind him and the locks fell in place.

I sat in my small room with the echoes of Ian's warnings. I laid down on the bed, not bothering to take off my boots, and tried to get some rest.

Whatever would happen this evening, whatever we walked into, I knew that I wouldn't be doing it alone. Clay would be at my side. And even though I wasn't quite sure what had happened, or what was going to happen, I knew one thing for sure: he wouldn't let me down. He wouldn't betray me, and he certainly wouldn't walk me straight into a trap.

If that wasn't true? If that one belief that I'd managed to uphold for these last few years proved to be false?

Then maybe it was just fine with me if I didn't come back from this mission.

21

By the time the door opened again, I'd managed to rest, clean and stretch. I'd been offered some new clothing, and not just any type of clothing, either. Unless I was mistaken, this was some kind of light armor—a thin fabric, not Kevlar, which was uncomfortable and unstretchable as all get out—but something that felt just as resistant, while being lighter, more molded, and able to stretch and move with me.

I loved it, especially the fact that it was completely black.

The leader of the guild, Sonsil, stepped in. He was definitely older than twenty. He looked more like thirty, maybe even closer to forty. It was hard to tell, and it hardly mattered. He moved with the confidence of a trained warrior and the assurance that no one would challenge him in his castle. Even though he wasn't Traded due to his age, he wouldn't be someone to trifle with.

Not for now, anyway.

"Alone this time?" I asked with a slight smile that I hoped proved more disarming than threatening.

"Come with me," he said, ignoring my question.

Not having any better offers on my dance card, I followed him out into the corridor. There were a few people milling about, all of them dressed in the same ominous black, all of them making way for their leader. Some with reverence, others with fear.

Sonsil didn't seem particularly pleased or stressed by any of it, just walking down the hallway as though he owned the entire area and everyone in it. Which he probably did.

He opened the door and gestured for me to go in. I walked past him, not worried that he would stab me in the back. If he'd wanted me dead, he'd had ample opportunity to make it happen. I gasped when I looked inside the room. It wasn't a huge room, maybe ten feet by ten, but each wall was lined with weapons, like a tiny armory of dreams. There were guns, blades, daggers, even bows! I sucked at using bows, but thought they were the coolest range weapon ever.

"Pick your weapons for tonight," he offered.

I glanced at him and raised an eyebrow.

"We want the item back in one piece. We need to make sure that the people we send will be returning alive."

"Makes sense," I muttered, then grinned as I observed the different blades. I selected two long, thin swords, several daggers, two handguns, and this weird-looking blast gun, almost like a mix between an automatic weapon and a rocket-launcher. I wasn't exactly sure what it would do, but in a pinch, I imagined it would be handy. And fun!

I turned to face him.

"Good selection," he said.

"Thank you!" I smiled. "These are nice weapons. I see that you take your business seriously."

He nodded.

"What is your business, anyway?"

He looked distant all of a sudden. "We make sure that those who can affect others are kept in check."

"I'm sorry?" I said. He focused back on me and a slight smile tugged at his lips again.

"Some of the Traded are bad," he offered, simplifying his terms, although doing it in such a way that I didn't feel spoken down to. Now there was a trick. Certainly not something that the teachers at my school had mastered. "So we make sure that the bad ones don't get to hurt other Traded, or humans."

"Oh?" I said. "That seems like a pretty good idea."

"It is," he offered. "It's a tenuous alliance that we have. There's a balance to be maintained, after all. If too many Traded go bad and hurt their human counterparts, then the humans may lose patience with us."

"We are more powerful than they are," I countered.

"There are many more of them than us," he said, "and they have had twenty years to arm themselves against us. It would be foolish of us to think that we were in any bargaining position, nor in any position where we would take the humans by surprise."

I cocked my head and considered for a few moments.

"That does sound wise, I suppose." I said. "So, you're a Traded, then?"

Another slight smile. But no answer.

I pushed on. "And this is a guild?"

"We are. One of many. Just like the fighter's league that your friend brought the item to."

"So why don't you just negotiate with them to get it back?" I said.

His eyes darkened. He could certainly be moody. "We much prefer not being seen, and negotiations require stepping up to the bargaining table. And that might get us noticed by the wrong people."

"The wrong people being human, or Traded?" I asked, hitting my stride.

"That is something only the higher representatives of our guild get to know. Are you ready?"

Question period had apparently ended. But I knew more than I had beforehand, and that would have to do.

"Ready as I'll ever be," I said, and followed him out of the armory.

Ian waited outside. The leader nodded to him, nodded to me, and then left in such a way that made it clear he didn't expect either one of us to follow.

"You have everything you need?" Ian asked.

"I think so."

"Here." He handed me several energy bars. I threw them into my pack.

"Might come in handy if you get hungry along the way."

"Thanks," I offered him a smile. "So this place isn't so bad, is it?"

He began walking down the corridor, leading me towards wherever I needed to be. I imagined he led me towards Clay.

"Depends what you mean by bad, I suppose," Ian said, selecting his words carefully.

"Well I mean, it's a guild. It seems as good as any, and it seems to play an important role in the ecosystem of humans to Traded. That's a good thing, right?"

"They kill people like us." Ian said after a moment of reflection.

"Well, just the bad ones," I whispered. "Someone has to deal with them. I mean, it's a fine balance, right? Traded are more powerful and have different abilities than humans, but there are so many more humans who are armed to the teeth and know how to deal with us, because they've had so much time to analyze us and study us and train us, and bring us up. It seems like a fair trade-off."

"Does it?" Ian asked.

"Well, it does," I shrugged. "I mean, we have all these skills, and talents, and abilities. Why not use them to keep the world safer?"

Ian glanced sideways at me, as though waiting for me to come to a conclusion on my own. But it was a conclusion that I certainly wasn't reaching. He seemed to give up after a few moments.

"Did you ever wonder why they trained you to fight?" he asked. "I mean, the teachers at the schools—they were human, right? So, why would they train you to fight? If they were so scared of the Traded, why would they teach them about weapons? Why would they teach them about combat techniques? And why would they teach them to sneak around and handle their powers? Did you ever consider that?"

"I can't say that I have..." he did make a fine point. Why would they teach us all of those skills if they wanted to keep us in check? I wrapped my head around everything I'd learned. "And the guilds are also human creations," I stated.

"They have to be," he agreed. "Every Traded is less than twenty years old, and the guilds have been in preparation for years."

"But they existed before now?"

Another nod. "These were created specifically to keep Traded in line. And some guilds focus on keeping *all* Traded in line."

"So maybe the humans just felt that they needed some extra firepower?" I offered. "Maybe all that they needed were Traded who were trained to keep other Traded in check. Like you said, a lot of us have powers, which could be destructive. Isn't it better than genocide, at the end of the day? To teach us to keep ourselves and humans safe? Instead of just killing us all, because they can't contain us?"

Ian grew silent. I thought maybe the conversation had ended, but I was wrong.

"So who gets to be judge, jury and executioner?" he asked. "How do we decide who's big and who's bad, if most of the Traded have been trained to fight, and have been locked away in schools or in guilds for years, with few touchpoints to the world outside and to humanity? How do we get to decide who's bad, or who just has to learn better?"

I mulled that for a while as we walked. A few more

people passed by. They gave Ian a wide berth. Ian looked pretty grumpy, so I backed their play.

"Maybe there just isn't time," I said. "Maybe things would get out of hand too quickly, so they have to err on the side of safety."

"I'm not sure that's the right side to err on," Ian immediately said. "What if they decided that you were bad? Or me? Or worse, what if you had to come after Clay?"

"They didn't kill him, though," I said, my limbs growing cold. "They just locked him up. As soon as he retrieves the thing he stole, then he'll be fine, right? They're giving him a chance to make amends. That's a good thing to do—give him a chance to learn..." my voice drifted away.

Ian didn't add anything else. He'd made his point though. But I'd made mine, too. It would just be a matter of observing and paying attention, and seeing how the dice rolled around us.

"Look, I'll meet you shortly. Just keep going forward and you'll see Clay. Don't try anything, Tira." He made sure he had my attention before continuing. "Don't ever think they're not watching."

"They?" I asked, raising an eyebrow. He nodded, as though pleased that I'd gotten it, and turned down another corridor. I watched him go, shook my head, and continued down the first hallway.

This whole quandary wasn't so much about black

and white, as it was about all the shades of grey in between. And that was a much harder territory to navigate. All I wanted to do at the end of the day though, was to keep Clay safe.

If I just had one target—one goal in mind—I hoped that it would make it easier to accomplish.

22

I JOINED up with Clay and we fist-bumped, avoiding another awkward hug. We stood before two large double doors, which I hadn't seen before. Unless I was mistaken, which I very well might have been, we were almost a block to the west from where we'd originally entered.

Clay looked good. Sleep had done wonders for him, as it always did. His right eye was fully opened and barely looked bruised. He'd cleaned up and wasn't covered in blood anymore. Dressed in black from head to toe, his dark skin seemed a little bit lighter. His eyes, however, seemed much darker, and his grin all that much more prominent.

He was enjoying this. He was absolutely loving every minute of this, even though I'd been terrified of losing him all this time.

Of course he was, and why wouldn't he be? We were heading into another mission, probably a battle. Battles were by far his favorite. And he'd certainly grabbed enough weapons to take on several people at once.

"Shall we?" Clay said, indicating the door with a flourish.

Anticipation began to grow in me.

We stepped out into the street. We were definitely west from where I'd entered, and several streets away. How big was this underground complex? And how much more of it was there?

The day had stretched into evening, the sun low on the horizon. Clay walked confidently west, as though he knew where to go. Which he probably did, considering he was the one who'd stolen the item.

I sensed a familiar presence to my right, where a third shadow joined us. Ian had reverted back to dog form, although he seemed more of a wolf than a dog this time. When he looked at me, I had no doubt that it was him. The eyes were the giveaway. The eyes were always the same, maybe not in shape or color, but in depth and warmth.

I gave him a slight grin. Clay noticed the canine walking beside me.

"Friend of yours?" he said.

"Yeah," I answered, "his name's Ian."

It took a little bit of self-control not to call him

Max. I might still call him Max from time to time when it was just the two of us, but that was for us only. Ian glanced my way, and his eyes narrowed a bit. Perhaps with suspicion, or perhaps gratitude. I was willing to assume gratitude in this case.

I reached down and patted his head was we walked forward. I didn't really know much about Ian yet, but I did know one thing: he was willing to walk beside me, no matter what. That counted for a lot.

Alright, it wasn't just going to be Clay and me. I hated to admit it, but I felt better for having Ian there. Clay had been erratic and had kept secrets from me. I mean, he always had, but the stakes had never been this high before. I still believed he wanted what was best for me, but he needed to involve me a bit more.

A lot more, in fact.

And I wasn't exactly sure what we were headed into, but I did know that it was Clay's doing. Whatever choices he'd made trying to join this particular fighter's league, he wasn't very good at thinking things through. Too enthusiastic, I guess.

The street around us stretched in quiet shadows and a few streetlights. It seemed we didn't have far to go since we were walking. But, if the two guilds were so close to each other, why not just swarm them? Why send in two unknowns? Unless they didn't want to reveal who tried to take back the item.

Of course. Sonsil had said that he didn't want them

to know who appropriated the canister. We were a plan, at best. A deniability, at worse.

Clay suddenly stopped and turned to face me. I did the same. I could only see regret in those eyes—an emotion I'd not seen etched across his features in our many years of friendship.

"Look, I'm really sorry you got caught," he said, breathless. "I saw you go down, and I knew enough to know that they weren't going to kill you, and I was going to come back for you!"

His words hit me like ten pounds of sharp bricks.

"You mean you left me there?" I said softly. "I thought that you'd gotten captured there, which is why you couldn't bring me with you."

His hand went up to his head, as though trying to fight off a headache, or like he regretted his actions, or maybe just because a fly was there...I couldn't tell anymore.

"Well, I mean, I would have, if I'd have stayed longer," he said. "But I knew enough about them to know that they wouldn't kill you, and that they'd just keep you somewhere, and I was going to come back as soon as I delivered the canister to the fighter's league. I figured you could just sleep off the knock you got on the head, and I couldn't carry everything out..."

"You left me there?" the words seemed foreign to my tongue. "And you carried the item you'd come to steal instead?"

He looked flustered. My immediate reaction was to back away, to just leave Clay alone because we were friends and it had always been just the two of us, so I couldn't push him with this. Usually, I would have backed down.

But not today. Not for this. Not now.

Not anymore.

I held my ground. Ian nuzzled my left hand where it dangled by my side, and I placed it gently on his head. I wasn't alone, and Clay wasn't alone either. We were here. But he had to trust Ian and I if we were going to survive this.

Hell, I had to trust Clay, too, and I just didn't know if I could right now. Not without answers that I didn't necessarily want to hear.

"I screwed up," Clay said. He took a deep breath, as though making a tough decision. "Look, I'm not supposed to tell you anything, Tira." My eyes widened, but he pushed on. "That was the deal all along. We go on missions. Sometimes tests. I don't mention anything to anyone."

"Why?" I asked softly.

"I don't know, but I knew what was promised. We'd get to go in the same league together. We wouldn't be separated."

"But you left me."

"Only because I needed to get them the canister before our two weeks were up or we'd be separated, and I knew you wouldn't be killed. They promised that, too. And they've always kept their promises, Tira, you *have* to believe me."

I mulled over that. A dog barked in the distance, then the world returned to silence. I fought the urge to wrap the shadows around me and leave Clay and Ian behind.

"I do believe you," I said softly. "But we can't afford to keep secrets from each other anymore." I held his eyes. "Deal?"

He looked relieved. "Deal."

"So, what was in the canister?"

"I'm not sure," he said, seeming to find firmer ground again. "But, look, Tira, they say that they can build a portal with the stuff in them. A portal back to the worlds of the Traded."

I stood a little straighter and narrowed my eyes.

"I'm not making this up," he said, holding up his arms defensively. "Look. They say that they can build a portal and send some Traded back. Some people don't want us to use them, because they don't know what else they might bring back out here. But, I mean, as far as I'm concerned, it might bring those human kids back too, right? Everybody gets to go home! And, I mean, Tira," he took my hands in his, held them like they were his lifeline, "you've been wanting to go home and find your own kind forever! I could just go with you. I don't care about my people. But you seem to! I thought…" He gripped my hands more tightly, "I thought that I was doing something good, that I could help myself, maybe find the fighter's league, and then through them I could help you get a portal and get home. And I swear, I didn't think you'd get in any more trouble there. I swear that I thought you were going to be safe for the time being, and I would have come back for you."

He paused, spoke more softly, looked me in the eye in a way that sent shivers down my spine. "I will *always* come back for you."

I looked into his eyes, felt the pressure of his hands on mine, remembered all my years with Clay. He was always brash, yes. He didn't always think things through, no. But he always *did* come back for me. He never abandoned me anywhere, and he pushed me to be faster and better. To be more than what I would have been otherwise.

"I believe you," I whispered. He leaned in, my eyes wide as he came closer.

Then Ian gave a strangled dog cough, and Clay stood straight again. Ian pressed against my leg. I could hear his warning to be careful.

"We're not in school anymore," I told Clay gently. "This is a big bad world, and I don't think we know it as well as we think we do. I'm not sure about the guilds or the leagues. I'm not sure that what you're telling me right now is true, either," I pushed on, even though he looked stricken again. "But I do know that you didn't tell me about the league badge that you received."

I pulled it out of my pocket and gave it back to him.

"Why didn't you tell me?" My voice broke a bit.

Clay and I weren't exactly used to being vulnerable with each other, but we couldn't indulge in secrets anymore. We weren't just doing heists on human buildings with some boring old technological defenses. No. We were heading into another league filled with Traded who had trained, probably better than us, to take on any challenge that came their way.

Clay looked down at the medallion in his hand, and I could see a yearning in him that I'd rarely seen. Yearning to belong to something greater than himself. Heck, a chance to belong to *something*, and not just be scorned or hated. Clay loved a good fight. He was good at it. He had trained for it. That crest represented what he desired. And after living a life where your own desires were so secondary to everyone else's, could I blame him for pursuing it blindly?

"I just thought I could be a part of something," he said. "And I just didn't know if that was something I wasn't supposed to tell you, either."

How much more aren't you telling me, Clay?

The dog barked again in the distance, and we had a mission to accomplish. Time was running short. Clay needed to focus. Hell, *I* needed to focus, so we'd survive. We'd chat more later. We'd have a *hell* of a long chat, in fact, without Ian listening in. Just Clay and I, like it used to be.

"Okay," I said, surprisingly unemotional. But it had been a day of emotions. How many emotions could I spend in one day? Surely it was a limited currency.

He grinned and pocketed the medallion, then he absent-mindedly reached up to touch the locket held by a thick black cord at his neck, a nervous tick that showed he intended to focus on the moment. Clay was centering his thoughts, focusing on the mission at hand.

I just had to worry about finding my own focus now. Clay wasn't the perfect friend, no, but we hadn't been raised in the perfect environment, so I guess that was to be expected. He was willing to make sure that there would always be room for me wherever he went. And I knew that he would always come back for me.

And I would always come for him, too. Hadn't I proved that already? That was worth something. It was worth a lot, in fact. Friendships like that couldn't easily be replaced.

I grinned, feeling lighter for the first time since leaving the Margrave Academy.

I met his eyes and held them, felt Ian against my leg, a solid presence which grounded me.

"So, what's the plan?" I asked.

He grinned and, for a few moments, all felt right in the world once more.

23

WE WALKED for another twenty minutes before Clay stopped us near a busy intersection. I twitched at the urge to draw shadows to me. I exchanged a quick look with Ian. He'd been quiet since I'd had the whole exchange with Clay.

Clay pointed to the left, on a large four-laned street with quite a bit of traffic, even though we neared midnight. The street lamps were plentiful, the tall buildings still illuminated despite the late hour. Most of the office buildings were empty—giant high-rises that reached up to the sky with their ambition and profits.

"It's the third building on the left," Clay whispered. I glanced at the squatter building, nestled between two big constructs of steel and glass. The targeted building seemed older, lined with bricks and stucco. Intricate details made it stand out, which I loved, but I hated the fact that it had few windows, so I couldn't see inside that easily. It seemed a little bit more secure because of the lack of windows, although I wasn't really sure how secure the newer buildings were, either. Probably full of traps.

Everything was always full of traps.

"Where are they in the building?" I asked. Clay shrugged, which was exactly the answer I'd expected. Then he grinned, which was the second answer I'd expected.

"I'm going to go in," he said, "and I'm going to grab the canister and meet you outside. And you just keep an eye out to make sure that the exit stays clear."

It was a plan that we'd done several times before, sure. But it didn't feel right. Not now. Not at this point. And not with the amount of danger we might potentially be facing.

"I think we should stick together," I said. Ian made a little sound beside me that indicated he agreed.

Clay shook his head. "Too dangerous. They know me. What if you get caught? What if they figure me out? At least this way, you can get help and come find me."

"Get help? Who would I get help from?" I gave a strangled laugh. "Clay, you're my only friend. Well, you and Ian." I added quickly, when he made another little noise. "But we're in this together, Clay. We said that we'd go in together, and I'm not leaving you alone now."

"Alright," he looked frustrated. "But, look. I'm not sure what kind of reception we're going to get here. They already know me, so I'm thinking I might just be able to walk in there, say 'hey,' grab it and get out. They don't know you, so we're going to have more questions to answer if you're there."

"How well do they know you?" I asked.

He shrugged. "We did a lot of heists for them. I mean, all of them."

Ian coughed again and Clay gave him a nasty look.

"They're not bad, Tira! That test the other day? That was for them. So they know some of what you can do. And they know we're tight!"

"Clay, if we've been working for this guild all this time, and they even tested us, remember that you got an emblem, and I didn't," I said softly. "I don't think they want me, Clay."

"Well, they're wrong," his voice echoed and he lowered it again, though anger laced every word. Several cars went by, and I held my hood closer to my head. I felt so exposed at this intersection. Clay instinctively stepped between me and the passersby, sensing my discomfort. The kindness of the gesture, the easy familiarity, formed a lump in my throat.

"They're going to separate us, Clay," I whispered, which he somehow heard despite a rumbling bus.

"No, they won't," he said, grabbing my upper arms again. "I promise you. They won't separate us. We'll find a way."

He was so confident that I nodded and swallowed the lump. Either way, we had to deal with this, first, or neither of us would be joining a league.

"I'm not going to wait for you outside," I whispered. "I'll stick to the shadows, sure, but there's no way I'm letting you go in there alone, Clay."

"I wish you would," he said, not looking at me, but at the building up ahead.

"Listen," I said, "we're in this together. We always have been, we always will be, right?"

He sighed. "Yeah," he said, "we are. Just be careful in there. I don't want to see you get dropped again."

"Oh," I said, raising an eyebrow, "*I'm* the one we're worried about getting dropped here? Who got dropped during the so-called test, Mr. I-Got-A-Guild-Invite?"

He laughed, and I felt lighter by the time we approached the building. The wide sidewalk provided little cover, but the streetlight grew sparse. Clay looked around, made sure no cars were incoming. He pulled out a gun with a silencer on it, a model I couldn't quite make out in the darkness, and fired at the next streetlight. It went out in a shower of glass, plunging us in darkness.

"I'll be right behind you," I told Clay, squeezing his arm.

"I know," he nodded, wisps escaping his ponytail, refusing to be contained. He vibrated with excitement and purpose as he walked toward the steps leading to the stone building. I watched him go, confidently stepping into the light of the building as I lingered in the darkness.

A familiar head butted my hand.

"Stay close to me," I whispered to Ian.

I folded the shadows around us, the night becoming crisper, the air clearer, the world safer. No one else controlled these shadows, as they bent to my will and gladly slipped around me, like an old friend greeting me with a warm cup of tea on a cold day.

My fingers were threaded in Ian's warm fur. I looked down into his eyes, and we walked quickly to catch up to Clay, who'd reached the entrance. Even in the light I could feel my shadows holding tight, intent on not letting me go.

We reached Clay just as he yanked the door open. I sucked in my breath. He heard me and grinned my way.

"It's a fighter's league!" he whispered. "Do you really think they're scared of anyone just coming in here and taking advantage of them?"

Ian sniffed the air and took a step in front of me. Clay walked in, and Ian and I followed a little bit behind.

The door led directly to stairs leading up and down.

Clay headed up, without hesitation, toward the well-lit top corridor. I struggled to find enough shadows to keep both Ian and I hidden, glad that Clay cast a decent shadow himself. I looked at his shadow, through the ones dancing around me, remembering the shifting shadows that I'd lost control of.

His shadow seemed thin. The old tiled floor at his feet didn't seem as dark as the shadow should make it. But the shadow didn't shift in any unexpected way.

"Hey, I'm back!" he shouted in his convivial manner with his deep, gruff voice. It snapped me back to the moment, and away from staring at shadows.

Clay entered a large room. Three people looked up smiling, apparently glad to see him. They all approached him as they greeted him. I hung back, so they didn't accidentally bump into me.

The first to reach him was a tall woman, a blonde with dark skin, hair in a ponytail reaching down past her hips. She wore about a hundred shiny bracelets, and I was jealous of every single one of them. She seemed genuinely happy to see Clay and hugged him. He hugged her back, and it didn't seem awkward.

I narrowed my eyes and stared at her.

The second one was a short man, hair so pale as to be almost white, although I didn't think he was old. He seemed our age, and so was probably one of the Traded. His eyes stood in deep contrast to his pale hair and face. Not black, like Clay's, though. More like smoky dark. Like at one point he'd been caught in a burning building, and some of that smoke had remained trapped in his head, peering out through the thin film of his eyes. That wasn't a comforting thought.

I glanced to the third person. I thought this one might be human, although it was hard to tell. Truth be told, I much preferred how different Traded looked. It proved much easier to tell them apart. Because I found this one generic-looking, I figured that they must be completely human. Straight, red hair, narrower eyes, wide smile, muscled arms. But I might be completely wrong, because I based it on absolutely nothing but what I could see. It's not like any of them wore a badge or obviously looked like a purple-skinned demon.

When I looked at Clay among them, I realized that he could pass too, if he really wanted to. His eyes were just a little bit too covered in darkness, but even then, a good pair of sunglasses and nobody would know he was Traded. He could hide the claw-like shape of his hands with gloves, and not smile so no one would notice the strange sharpness of his teeth.

He could slip into society and just vanish, become one of them, not have to go home, not long to find a place that would accept him for who he was, and for what he looked like.

I was the one who wanted that. To find a home with others like me. Not him, because he could fit in here. Still, he hunted for ways to form a portal home. To *my* home. I watched him chat with his friends and realized that he was doing that for me. He had a home here, but he still thought of me, and what I might want.

I couldn't believe I'd ever doubted him. I couldn't believe I'd doubted my oldest friend, just because I got knocked on the head and he had to make a tough call to leave me behind.

I pressed further against the wall where the shadows were thickest, and kept them surrounding Ian and I. Clay exchanged pleasantries with the others, and then they encouraged him to go through to speak to someone they called "the boss."

Clay laughed and smiled and shook hands with all of them, and then he stepped through the door, making sure to hold it open a little longer, sharing a few more words with the three. I passed by the tall blonde woman, smelled her perfume of roses. So Earth-like a scent, revolting in its sweetness.

Past the door stood desks and offices with big windows, and old carpets and campaign posters from elections long passed. Not exactly what I'd expected from a fighter's league, but I guess each guild had to make do with what they were given.

Clay walked with more confidence than I expected he might. He greeted each person warmly, the office area extremely busy for being night time. I guessed that fights took place at night.

Most people here looked human, and I couldn't

easily spot a Traded among them. An old pink-sweatered grandmother walked past me, patted Clay on the back, and even gave him a cookie.

Shit, this place wasn't half bad. I could see why Clay liked it. Everyone seemed warm and friendly, and there were cookies! I wanted a cookie. I considered stealing one, though I decided against it, struggling to stay out of the way while keeping the shadows folded against Ian and I. Clay glanced back for half a second, worry flickering across his face. A woman walked behind me, missing me by a few inches. I called the shadows more densely around me.

This was going to be impossible. The overhead lights were too strong and there were too many people. Somebody would detect me. Clay had been right, I should have stayed outside.

No.

I just had to alter my environment to suit me. I pulled out a metal star and swung it at one of the overhead lights, managing not to hit the actual bulb, which would have sent it exploding, but the socket on the side instead. The light flickered out, plunging a third of the corridor in darkness. I breathed more easily. A few people stopped walking and looked up, puzzled.

"This old building..." the grandmother said, "I swear, every day it just needs more and more repairs."

Clay said something to her and kept walking. A few

others greeted him and kept going on their way as well, and it seemed that everybody decided to dissipate away from where the shadows had fallen. Maybe they understood that something lurked within them. They were right, something did. And that something was growing damn irritated at all the foot traffic here.

I trailed after Clay, who was now a bit ahead of us, Ian sticking close to me. We reached another part of the corridor, still covered in ugly carpet, a few half cubicle walls marking off office spaces. I shuddered at their grayness, remembering the walls separating our cells.

Clay grabbed the handle of the door at the end. He glanced back my way and gave a subtle nod. He couldn't see me returning it, but I found comfort in the fact that he knew I still followed him. That he knew I would still be there like I said I would be.

He opened the door and headed in without hesitation. I walked closer to slip in, but before I could, the door closed behind him.

He hadn't been nodding to be comforting. He'd been nodding to tell me to wait here. *Wait here while I go and get the thing. Stay behind like was my original plan.*

Something nudged my leg, and I realized that Ian was trying to get my attention. I turned and saw a slew of Traded walking into the office area, each looking meaner than the last. Fighters to the core, ripped with muscles, weapons, and confidence.

They were heading straight for me, in a narrow corridor, and there were few shadows in which to hide.

I quickly doubled back before they could reach us, Ian sticking close. I passed near the burnt-out light and slipped into an office. The fighters walked past me, none the wiser.

My blood ran cold. One was shorter and sported blue hair. Had he been the man who'd attacked us in the halfway house? I made a note to check on that later. Maybe much later, as it didn't seem to be a priority right now. Still, I stared at him as he and a few other fighters headed into the room where Clay had vanished. A few fighters unfortunately stayed near the offices, hanging out and chatting.

I placed my hand on Ian's head as though to calm him, but it was more to calm myself. I could feel vibrations flowing from him. He was as alert as I was. Something wasn't quite right, and I couldn't tell what.

Clay had gone in and I had to trust that he was safe, and my job was to keep an escape path open. But with all those fighters here…why the hell were they all here? What even was this place?

"Cookie?" a wavering voice asked, and I turned around, surprised to find the grandmother right beside me, holding up the plate of cookies. I opened my mouth, but no words came out.

She can see me?

Ian growled. The grandmother raised the cookie

plate and a gun lay under it. Not suffering from the same hesitation I did, Ian leapt at her. He yelped, yanked back by an unseen force and smashed against the wall.

"Ian!" I screamed, dropping the apparently dysfunctional shadows. I reached for my sword, but my arm wouldn't move, like it was trapped in thick molasses. None of my body would move.

I'd felt that force before. I managed to glance toward the door.

"Hey, demon," Blake said, looking as smug as he ever had, holding me and Ian in place. If he gave me an inch, I'd make him pay.

He wanted a demon? I could be that, just for him. I'd rip his damn eyes out and feed them to him, so this demon would be the last sight he saw on this cursed planet.

I SHOULDERED THE DOOR AGAIN, but it held annoyingly fast. Damn office door! Here I thought this building was less secure. I couldn't have been more wrong.

They'd taken Ian. They'd taken my weapons, *again*, and they'd left me here, Blake grinning at me like it was all a joke he'd played on me. Worse: I'd never found out what that giant gun did. This was the cheese grater all over again.

I kicked the door, bounced off, crossed my arms and stared at it.

How the hell was I supposed to get out of here? Where was Clay? Where had they taken Ian?

"Hey!" I screamed. Nobody answered. Of *course* nobody answered.

How had they been able to see me through my

shadows? Why were my powers, which had been so useful when I was at school, now suddenly so useless?

Because I wasn't in school anymore. Because I was in the real world, where people knew how to use their powers for different purposes, and not everybody had gone to the schools and just met the same people over and over again. And there were people out here—other Traded—who could in fact see me for what I was. Spot me easily, whereas nobody could beforehand.

My limbs grew cold as I uncrossed my arms and stared at the door, helpless.

But how had they even known I was here? Did I trip some kind of trap or alarm? Did they just see me? I didn't think so—I'd made it pretty far. Why let me get this far? Did someone in the other guild betray us? That seemed unlikely...they wanted the canister back. They were the ones who'd sent us here in the first place, after all.

Another possibility began to tug at me, and I tried to ignore it, not liking it one bit. It begged to be considered though. *Clay.* Maybe it *had* been Clay. Maybe Clay was so obsessed with the possibility of joining this fighter's league that he'd been willing to just cast me aside. They had found me after he'd stepped away from us, after all. If they'd *known* to look for me...

Just as I began to wrap my mind and heart around the possibility of betrayal, the door opened and Clay stepped in. He closed the door behind him and had the decency to look embarrassed.

"Look, I'm sorry," he said. "I just didn't know how else to get you away safely from that guy, Ian."

"Where is he?" I asked, ignoring the apology.

"He's safe enough," Clay said.

I shot him a look.

"I mean, he *is* safe. He's locked up," he looked at me, a plea in his eyes. "He's dangerous, Tira."

"*He's* the dangerous one?" I raised an eyebrow.

"He is. He's part of the Guild of Shadows. They're assassins, Tira! All they do is kill people, and hide bodies, and stuff like that."

"They're not the ones holding me prisoner right now," I said, ice dripping from my words, surprised at the anger I felt toward Clay.

"You're not a prisoner," Clay said. "It's a fighter's league. They fight. Mostly amongst themselves, like gladiator-style combat. And sometimes others, depending on who's organizing what. But they don't go out there and just kill people. That's not what they do. All they do is fight here and there," he tried a grin on me. "You know I love a good fight!"

He needed me to tell him it was all okay. I could see it—from the dropping of his shoulders to him barely meeting my eyes. But I couldn't do that. Not just yet.

"I want to make sure Ian is okay," I said. "He came to keep me safe, after all."

"Did he?" Clay asked. "Tira, he probably just came to get the canister, kill the two of us, and then make off. Or to keep an eye on us, at best! Like I said, these aren't nice people. You're putting your trust in the wrong place."

I didn't answer. I wasn't sure anymore where I should put my trust.

"Is Blake part of this fighter's league?"

"Nah," Clay said. "Not sure what his deal is. I've been told not to worry about him. But he's definitely not part of this league. Maybe another league visiting? I don't know. Anyways, he's still a jackass."

I smiled a bit at that, but that smile quickly faded.

"How did they know I was here?" I asked. "They could see through my shadows, like they did in the Guild of Shadows."

Guild of Shadows. My tongue wrapped nicely around that. Was it really a guild of assassins? They hadn't hidden that from me. They said that they kept things in check, sure. There was a difference between just going out to kill people and going out to kill people who were going to make things worse.

It was a pretty damn big difference in my mind.

"I don't know," Clay said, looking bewildered by that as well. "I honestly didn't think they'd see you. I mean, I knew you'd have to reveal yourself eventually, but I was going to let you do that on your own. Just kind of lay the groundwork for you, and then you could just show them what you were capable of, and they'd let you join the fighter's league with me, and that would be that. But I don't know how they were able to tell where you were. I couldn't see you!"

"Why didn't you let me step into the door with you at the end of the hallway?"

I'd never seen Clay flush bright red before, but apparently it was possible. It made him look even more human.

"Well, the boss, she doesn't like it when there are surprises."

"The boss?" I asked, raising an eyebrow.

He shrugged. "Yeah, I guess it was silly, but I figured if I pissed her off with you, then the chances of you joining were gone. But if you waited in the corridor and then I let you in when it made more sense or when she was more willing to listen, or something..." He shrugged again. "I don't know. I guess I didn't really think it through."

"I guess you didn't," I agreed. "It still doesn't answer how they found me."

"No. But we're not in school anymore, Tira. The world is different out here. There are people with more power, and more dangerous than we thought they might be. That's why we've got to stick together, right?"

He looked at me with his wide eyes. He was so keen on joining a fighter's league. He'd always wanted to join a fighter's league, since he'd found out they existed. Refining his skills to be able to take them on.

But me? I'd never selected a guild. I'd never selected a path. Part of me always believed I'd just follow Clay wherever he went. And isn't that what I was doing right now? Following him here to the fighter's league?

Why was it so hard for me to just commit to this, and follow his plan? He really wanted me to. He wanted us to stay together. Isn't that what I wanted?

"Want to watch me fight?" Clay asked suddenly to break the silence. He didn't like it when we fought. Can't say I blamed him. It had happened rarely, but I'd hated it every single time.

"You're going to take part in a fight?" I asked, a bit curious.

"Sure," he said. "I've already fought a few times. I mean, that's partly how they test you, right? There's going to be a bigger one tonight, biggest one I've taken part in, and you can watch."

"Okay," I said. "But I want to see Ian, too. Make sure he's safe."

Clay looked a little bit hurt at the suggestion that Ian wasn't safe. But he still nodded.

"Don't go in the shadows," he said. "Just stay with me and you'll be fine. Don't try anything. Don't steal anything. And don't vanish. Whatever happens here, they see and they know. Might as well be upfront about it."

"We still need to get that canister, Clay," I said, trying to keep him on track. I knew that we'd spent our entire lives preparing to join a guild, and we had limited time in which to do it, but I doubted the Guild of Shadows cared much about that. Clay had to focus on more than one thing, and I wasn't sure he could do that. It's part of what made him so good in battles—his unshifting focus on winning.

But, out here? I didn't think it was doing him any favors. He'd have to expend his focus fast, or we'd both end up paying the price.

"We will," he said. "You'll get a chance to scout things out while you watch the fight, and we'll make a plan after. Deal?"

I nodded and followed him out of the office. We didn't go very far before Clay opened up another office. A cage contained a very annoyed looking Ian.

"Ian," I said. He stayed seated in the cage and stared at me, his eyes narrowing. "Are you alright?" I asked.

"They think he's just a dog," Clay said. "Mean son of a bitch wolf. But just a dog. I didn't tell them." He looked from Ian to me, seeming proud that he'd managed to keep the secret. I guess it was something. If they knew he was a Guild of Shadows operative…who knew *what* they'd do to him.

"Do you have the key?" I asked. Clay nodded and barely hesitated before handing it to me. I popped the cage open. "Why would they bother locking a dog up?"

"Really, *really* mean wolf," Clay said, narrowing his eyes at Ian, who took a step out and growled, advancing towards Clay.

"It wasn't his fault," I said, standing between the two of them, focusing on Ian. "Clay didn't know that we were going to be ambushed like that. He certainly didn't mean for either one of us to get hurt. We just have to figure this out," I said, "find the canister and get out. That's it. That's what we came here to do, isn't it?"

I wished he was in his human form so that he could communicate with me, but instead he stopped growling and sat down, his ears slightly back. But he nodded.

"Good," I said. "Clay, where is the canister?"

"It's probably going to be with the boss," he said. "She's been keeping close tabs on it. And you'll see her at the fight. You probably won't be able to get close to her, but pay attention to the details. After the fight, we'll be able to figure out how to steal it."

"Okay," I said skeptically. "Still not very clear on why you have to fight, though." He shrugged again. He was really making a habit of it.

"It's what's expected here, remember? It's a fighter's league. They know you'll come watch me fight. They don't mind. It'll give you a good chance to have a look around, see what you can see."

"Like the stolen canister?"

"Exactly," he said. But I'd seen the hesitation in his

eyes. He wanted me to stay here and scope out the area and the fight.

"Clay," I said, "you know once we take that canister back, they'll probably not want us to stay here as members, right?"

"No, I get that," he said. "There are other fighter's leagues out there." He added after a moment, and then he flashed a grin at me. "Now, come on! I've got to get ready!"

He opened the door and stepped out. I glanced at Ian, who seemed to be giving me a knowing look of *I told you we couldn't trust him.* I sighed.

"Not you, too," I whispered, and then trailed after Clay to see this fight. Ian followed, looking about as pleased as I did about the whole thing.

I HADN'T EXPECTED that Clay would be fighting a woman three times his size, green-skinned, with four arms. She looked mean and angry, and about to tear him to pieces. Part of me wanted to root for her—girl power and all that—but another part of me was terrified that she was about to tear Clay to pieces.

But Clay moved pretty fast from one side of the ring to the other, and landed a few blows himself, though he took more than he gave. I tried to rip my gaze away from the arena, which was about one story below where I stood, the viewers' gallery all around it on the floor above. I leaned on the railing to keep an eye on Clay, and I also glanced to my left, where the so-called *boss*—noticeable from the fact that she was surrounded by well-suited guards—was dressed to the nines herself, and also sat on a metal chair with the engraved word 'boss' at the top of the seat.

Very classy, I thought. Did all guild bosses have some kind of throne? At least it made them easy to identify.

I couldn't see the canister beside her. Only one expensive-looking drink graced the gilded table to her left, some blue concoction which swirled with sparkles. She toyed with it more than she drank it. I couldn't blame her—it was the perfect drink with which to do that. She seemed to be staring not just at the combat below, which she had a prime view of, but also at the other fighters around her, judging those who watched, those who ignored the battle, and those who chatted amongst themselves.

Her eyes caught mine a few times, and I looked away quickly. I didn't like what I saw in them. I thought she was human—in fact I was sure she was, because she was at least in her fifties—but something about her made my skin crawl. Ian sat beside me, wagging his tail. I suspected that annoyance fueled the tail, not joy.

I focused back on Clay. The battlefield wasn't level. Obstacles and uneven ground had been added to make the combat more interesting, or at least resemble some terrible sixties sci-fi movie. Clay kicked himself off a hill and landed on the woman's head, managing to knock her off balance. But she recovered quickly using one of her arms to push herself back up, and the other three to grab a spear and throw it at Clay's head.

I gasped, but he managed to avoid it, swerving just in the nick of time.

I looked to the back of the room, where several counters spun and rotated with high numbers, now nearing a million. A money sign at the end of the row made it clear we were talking dollars. The numbers shone and increased. Several other screens showed viewers chatting about the combat.

I recognized enough to know it was social media, and it was busy. I was suddenly glad I'd never been on those—it went by scary fast. A cheer sounded across the arena as a great blow landed on Clay. A quick glance didn't betray the cheerer. Too bad—I'd have gladly thrown them into the pit.

Another cheer and I suddenly understood. Although there were a few participants here, the game was being broadcast elsewhere, bets were coming in, and the cheers could flow from the comfort of their own homes.

The more blows were traded and parried, the higher the counter went, easily passing the one million mark. Nearing five, in fact. That was a lot of money, and the boss seemed more and more pleased, leaning back in her chair and swirling her sparkly drink.

My blood ran cold. This was how this guild made its money—by pitting Traded against Traded for maiming or death. In this case, the word *death* was crossed off the fighting board, but I didn't like how close that board was to the money counter.

I imagined that word wasn't always crossed out.

I glanced down, ignoring the rising bets. The woman grabbed a rock—no, not a rock, more like a boulder—and hurled it at Clay. She was stronger and bigger, but she was slower. Clay jumped to the right, avoided the boulder, and then dashed toward her, pulling out a sword. He managed to nick her thigh, but it didn't bite very deep. Her skin was definitely not as squishy as a human's.

I leaned on the railing, looking back towards the bets. They neared eight figures, and the boss seemed happy about that. She looked at me again, and this time I didn't look away, fascinated by what I saw in her eyes. They were so cold. And calculating.

She held my gaze, and something changed in her face, a slow smile crossing her lips. I looked away, back down towards Clay, but when I looked up two seconds later, she was still looking at me as though gauging me.

And then she looked towards the bet counter.

I followed her eyes. My breath caught in my throat. The word *death* was no longer crossed out. A band of light erupted around the arena below, the red word dancing on a yellow background. Those lights reflected in Clay's eyes, and a grin pulled at his lips. I'd beat him up for that, if he survived.

I stared in fury back at the boss, and she held her glass toward me, as though toasting me.

I took a step toward her and two of her giant goons stood in my way. A low growl erupted from Ian's throat.

"You coward!" I hissed at the boss. I didn't have to speak loudly to be heard, despite the grunting below, the shouting from the battle, and the cheering from the unseen spectators. The entire atmosphere of the place became vibrant with the possibility of bloodshed. The social media board exploded with enthusiasm.

I didn't like this world one bit.

"We all have a role to play," the boss said in a crisp voice.

I heard a familiar grunt and looked down. Clay had taken a hit in the stomach and was doubled over. The other fighter walked towards him. The giant band of marketing light now shone deep red, bathing the arena in its blood light, except for the two white words flashing against the background: *death now*.

The other fighter spotted it (probably because it was impossible to ignore). I don't know if she was surprised or worried, but she certainly knew it was her or Clay. I couldn't blame her for walking toward him, picking up a rock big enough to smash his skull in, and accelerating her pace before he could recover.

I didn't even think about it. Ian barked twice as I

grabbed the railing and launched myself over it, targeting her head.

I mostly hit her, grabbing her hair and pulling her down with me, trying to roll out of her way as she landed down with a thud. She was faster than I'd thought she would be, and managed to grab my foot with one of her hands. I kicked out, but she twisted, and my ankle snapped.

I screamed and kicked out again, but she wasn't letting go. She stood over me with that crushing boulder. Her damn four arms were coming in handy!

Ian howled from above. The boulder went up. I tried to gather shadows, but knew it would be useless.

I braced for the blow that would kill me.

But then her eyes widened, and she slipped down to the ground. The rock fell with a thud near her as her eyes rolled back in her head. The crowd cheered wildly as she breathed her last, her eyes locked with mine.

"I'm sorry," I whispered. I hadn't wanted her to die. But I hadn't wanted Clay to die, either.

Clay knelt beside me, throwing aside his bloody sword.

"Are you alright?" he said, gritting his teeth and still holding his middle.

"I will be," I said. The roar of the crowd pummeled down on us. His eyes widened at the cheer, but he stayed at my side. I could tell he wanted to acknowledge the crowd. To ham it up. To let their cheers bolster him.

I couldn't deny him his lifelong dream. "Go on," I smiled as best I could. "Take your victory stand."

He squeezed my shoulder and stood up, looking like a kid at Christmas, like all of the toys and all of the goodies he'd ever wanted were right here, around him.

I stayed on the ground, holding my broken ankle, looking at the dead woman, looking at Clay holding up his arms in victory. Then my eyes caught Ian's, still trapped behind the barrier.

His gaze gave no room for interpretation. We needed to get out of here. We needed to get out of here fast.

But I just wasn't sure that Clay would be coming back with us.

DESPITE CLAY'S assurances that they'd take care of me, I was unceremoniously dragged through the back of the arena and into what they called the fighters' preparation area. It felt more like a tiny dungeon. It smelled like one, too, dank and humid. Dark walls surrounded a small bench, or what I supposed could pass as a bed with no mattress.

They dragged me in there with my broken ankle. I bit down the screams of pain that threatened to explode straight from my ankle and out of my throat. As if I'd give them that satisfaction. The guard on my left, an angry man with only one arm and eagle eyes, kept a close eye on me. But not close enough to see me swipe a switchblade from the guard on my left, the one with two arms and no eagle eyes. I slipped it up my sleeve.

They dropped me in the tiny room, not even on the bench. Ian slipped past them.

"Stupid dog," the two-armed jailer scowled and tried to kick him. Ian growled and bit the guy's leg. The guard yelped and his partner rolled his eyes at him.

"Let's go," he said, dragging his friend out and closing the door behind them.

Closed and locked.

This was getting to be a pattern. One that I wasn't overly fond of.

I pushed myself back towards the wall, straightened my legs, gritted my teeth, and examined my ankle. I almost passed out from the pain. Stars exploded in front of my eyes. I lowered my head, trying really hard not to puke, because I'd just be puking on myself, and that wouldn't help the smell of this place.

I gulped in deep breaths, let the ankle lay where it was. It didn't look too bad, when I opened my eyes again. Either my boot held the bone in place, or it had only been fractured and maybe not completely broken.

I'd felt it snap, though. I'd *heard* it snap.

As I looked at my ankle and debated unzipping my boot, it wasn't the broken bone that I thought of, but the dead eyes of the woman, the fighter who'd just wanted a chance in the ring. Who had been killed by the greed of others.

The nausea began to pass. Ian sat and leaned against me, as though to comfort me. My head in my hands, I leaned on him, taking deep breaths, closing my eyes to focus on nothing but his warmth, and my breath.

"I don't think I like this place," I mumbled. Ian gave a low whine and moved me gently off him. I opened my eyes. The dog body beside me began to shift and change. I looked away, not wanting to embarrass him.

"It's okay," he said. I looked his way, and he was wearing the same dark clothes he'd been wearing before.

I frowned.

"There are some clothes that will shift with me," he said, "it's just all so black and depressing."

"Oh," I answered, not quite sure what else to say.

"I think I can help with your ankle," he offered.

I was too tired to ask how, but he offered the information, out of what I assumed was kindness.

"I have the ability to shift the bones in my skin," he said, looking at my ankle. He crouched at my feet, leaving my boot on. Then he looked into my eyes. "This is probably going to hurt."

I closed my eyes and gritted my teeth.

His hands circled my ankle. It didn't hurt, so much as felt warm.

"So you think you can fix it?" I asked. "Maybe splint it?"

"I can do better than that," he whispered. "If I concentrate hard enough, sometimes I can get other people's bones to shift, just a little bit."

"Shift?" I barely got the word out before the pain exploded in my ankle. I think I screamed. I might have thrown up. I definitely passed out. I most definitely slumped to the ground.

It took me a few moments to come back to my senses. Definitely more than a few breaths. My stomach was tied in knots, but I was pleased to see that I hadn't puked on myself.

Ian removed his hands from my ankle. He looked pale himself, like *he* might throw up.

"Don't throw up on me," I said, my voice hoarse in my own ears.

"You okay?" he asked. I wasn't sure how to answer that. I felt like I'd gotten hit by a truck—and that had happened once, so I knew what that felt like. This felt a little bit worse, in fact. Like something had reached inside me and changed a piece of me. I knew exactly what that piece was, too, and would walk on it for the rest of my life.

I pushed myself back up, leaning against the wall. My two legs were still stretched out in front of me, the dark leather boots clinging to them. I took a deep breath, and then rotated the ankle. It moved without complaint. Maybe a little bit of discomfort and stiffness that hadn't been there before, but that was it.

"You healed it!" I said, surprised. "You managed to fix my bone!"

He gave me a tired smile. "I wasn't sure I could," he said, "but I'm glad it worked."

"What am I, a guinea pig?" I said jokingly.

"No, but *I* could be one!"

I laughed. I hadn't heard him make a joke before. It suited him. He stopped smiling, and I noticed how exhausted he looked, his features gaunt and pale, even his brown hair limp.

"I'm sorry," I said. "I'm sorry for dragging you into this."

"It's okay," he answered. He seemed to ponder his answer for a moment longer. I left him the space he needed to consider it, now starting to understand his beats and pauses. "You didn't drag me into anything," he continued, "I offered to come, remember?"

"Did you?" I retorted, remembering Clay's words. "Did you come here because you wanted to help, or did you come here because you had an ulterior motive?"

His eyes widened a bit in surprise, then he sighed. He moved slowly, practically crawling toward me, and leaned on the wall right beside me, extending his legs like mine.

I stared ahead and waited for him to answer.

"The Guild of Shadows is not a terrible place to be," he said. His voice was strong and soft all at once. He had the voice of someone who could tell you stories into the night, and you'd listen to them. It didn't even matter what he spoke of. He could read a recipe, and you'd still be interested in listening to him.

I closed my eyes and I listened, losing myself in the words.

"We try to keep the balance between the guilds and the leagues, between the Traded and the humans and, yes, some people pay with their lives for that. But it's rewarding work. Or it can be, at least."

"Do you kill a lot of people?" I asked, keeping my eyes closed, focusing on his words.

"I've killed some," he said, not hiding the fact, "but I don't regret killing any of them," he continued.

"You'll kill more?" I said.

"I imagine I will," he offered. "Does that bother you?"

"Not really," I said, slightly surprised at my own words. "At least you're not in denial about what you do." I paused, haunted by the dead fighter's eyes. "That girl in the arena died in front of me. I didn't want her to die."

I didn't know how to explain what I wanted to ask, but thankfully, Ian seemed to follow what I was saying.

"I don't think she deserved to die," he said. "She was just trying to survive, follow the rules of her league. The fact that they allowed her to die, well…that's the kind of place this is, I suppose."

"Clay will end up dying here," I said, certainty tight in my chest. Tears streamed down my cheeks, and I let them. Clay was my friend—my best friend. I didn't want him to die here.

Ian didn't say anything, letting the silence stretch comfortably around us.

"I have to get him out of here," I said. "I have to help him find another way."

A pause.

"He really wants to belong here," Ian said.

"He wants to belong to a fighter's league," I said. "Surely they can't all be this deadly."

"No, there are different ones," he said, his voice soothing. "But this is the biggest one. The one where the most glory is to be found, where the best fighters go."

That's what Clay would want. I didn't say it out loud, though. I didn't want Ian to know that part, because knowing that made me question everything.

I'd have to wonder if Clay had meant it when he said he'd be willing to go to another fighter's league. If Clay cared enough about his own life, and mine, to try his hand at something different. Or if Clay had just decided he'd fight here until he could fight no more. He'd get killed, sure, but at least he'd go down in some twisted form of glory.

I just wasn't sure. My tears stopped. I opened my eyes and looked at the locked door. I needed to find Clay. I needed to get answers from him. And I needed to get us both out of here.

"I know that the Guild of Shadows has its issues," Ian said, "and I'm not one to lie to myself about the black and white nature of some of the decisions we take, but don't fool yourself, Tira. This fighter's league? It's powerful, and they've got their eyes on Clay. They're not going to let him go that easily."

"Maybe," I whispered, "but neither will I."

I'm PRETTY sure I fell asleep for a bit, leaning against the wall. I was pretty sore by the time I woke up.

Ian was still there, knees brought up under his chin. He didn't look like he'd slept at all. It reminded me of Clay making sure I could sleep during our last night at the school. I really had to stop getting thrown in jail so my friends could sleep more.

Once Ian noticed I was awake, he looked my way.

"I should go," he said.

"I get that," I offered. "You should get out while you can."

"That's not quite what I meant," he said. "I should go and get the keys, maybe help you get out. I think I'm ready to shift again."

"You really can't shift sometimes?" I asked. He shook his head.

"No, and I'm not sure exactly what it depends on. Sometimes, it's more tiring than other times. Sometimes I can shift five times in one night no problem, and other times I can barely shift once. A few years ago I got stuck in animal form for a week because I just couldn't shift out of it for some reason."

"Oh?" I asked. "What was the animal form?"

"A snail," he said. I stifled a laugh. He frowned.

"Hey, it wasn't all that bad. You just sort of go around when you're a snail. There's not that many expectations of you. You've got a home, you can hide in there in comfort for almost a week. It wasn't that bad at all. Kind of restful, kind of quiet and peaceful. I might do that again now in fact! I could use some peace and quiet!"

"Well, there's an easy solution for that!" I muttered. "Just get away from me. I seem to just be attracting trouble lately."

"It's not you," he said. "It's being Traded in this world. You've been sheltered for too long in the school. You've forgotten what it's like out here."

"I don't think you can call that sheltered," I said. "I mean, they didn't exactly treat us well. They put us in modified cells to sleep. If we got out of line, things got painful. I mean, sometimes we managed to get out for a bit, but even then if they'd have found out, that would have hurt, too."

I looked his way, and he looked at me skeptically. He seemed to do that a lot.

"What?" I asked.

"You really think they didn't know?" he said. "You really think that they didn't know that you were sneaking out?"

"Well, no," my turn to be skeptical. "Of course they didn't. We'd have gotten in even more trouble if they had."

"*Tira.*" I don't think I'd ever heard my name said with such exasperation, and lots of people had said it exasperatedly before. "Of course they knew! They probably followed in some way and found out what you were doing! I mean, that's the whole point of the schools! It's a training ground for the leagues and the guilds, so they have to know what you're capable of before placing you!"

I cocked my head a little bit, thinking about what he'd said.

"Is that why we had so many fighting classes?"

His eyes grew even wider.

"Of *course* that's why you had fighting classes and you learned how to handle weapons. Why else do you think you had that? That's not exactly normal high school material!"

I shrugged. "I don't know what normal high school looks like. This is all I know! So what you're saying is that they pretty much know everything we've been up to since being at that school."

"That's exactly what I'm saying."

"Okay," I said, "so we have to try something different, then. Wait. If they know everything about us from school, if they've been studying us that closely, wouldn't they know that Clay is my best friend? Wouldn't they know that we'd do anything for one another?"

I didn't look at Ian, and he remained quiet, letting me work through it. "That means there's a reason that they're doing this. There's a reason that he received the guild invitation, and I didn't." It hit me like the boulder from the battlefield would have. "They're testing him, and his loyalty to the fighter's league."

"Everyone receives a guild invitation," Ian said quietly. I ignored him. I hadn't received one, but now wasn't the time to argue about it.

What would they do to test Clay's loyalty now? They'd kept me alive, so that was a good sign. Or was it? Just as I pondered the possibilities, the door unlatched.

"I won't be far," Ian said, and he shifted down into a mouse, scampering away just as the door creaked open. Thank goodness the door was sticky.

I wasn't overly thrilled to see Blake step in.

"Hey, Tira," he said.

"Hey, Blake." I stood up. He looked surprised.

"Ankle all better?"

I shrugged. "Maybe she just didn't do that much damage."

"Probably best that she's gone then," he said.

Before I could think better of it, I pulled out the switchblade that I'd stolen from the guard, flipped it out and flung it in the air. I caught him by surprise, and he didn't have the time to activate his power before the blade struck the side of his cheek and cut deep.

I followed it and managed to knee him in the gut. He doubled over. I brought my elbow down to strike him in the back of the head. But my elbow stopped an inch from his skull, in his perfectly coiffed blond hair, and I was flung back against the wall, unable to move.

He stood back up and caught his breath. His cheek was badly cut. A definite scar. *Good*, I thought, wishing I could voice it. He brought his hand to his cheek and pulled it away, fingers covered in blood. He gave me a look that made it very clear he hoped that I would soon die.

He held out his hand, moved his fingers as though beckoning me, pulling me to him, until I could smell his hot breath on my face.

"I'm going to enjoy this next part," he said. Then he slammed his hand down. I fell to my knees. My ankle hurt but didn't break again. I was about to get up and try to punch him, but my two original captors pulled me up as Blake made sure I couldn't fight back. The guard grabbed his switchblade, looking annoyed and embarrassed.

Eagle eyes gave him a fierce look. This time, they made sure to shackle my hands behind my back.

"Don't do anything that stupid again," Blake said, and then he got an evil grin. "I doubt that it'll matter much, anyways." He sighed as though a great burden had been placed on him. "I fear that I'm leaving today, so we won't meet again."

"The loss isn't mine," I said through gritted teeth.

"Bye, Tira," he said and vanished from my sight, headed to wherever snakes like him lived.

I was dragged down the hall unceremoniously, part of me wishing that I'd kept the switchblade to use at a more opportune moment, but a bigger part of me glad that I'd made that bastard bleed.

2 8

<hr>

By the time I'd found my bearings again, I realized that I was being dragged into the arena, but not ceremoniously or heroically. No fighter's walk for me.

They unshackled me and threw me through the gates, uneven ground beneath my feet. In more ways than one.

They'd changed the battlefield—to keep fighters on their toes, I supposed. A few sandy patches and some grass had popped up, and the hills had shifted. Some of the ground was muddy and looked slippery as hell. There were no boulders, though, so that was nice.

I looked up towards where the boss sat. From her seat, she could see down into the arena at every angle. I glared at her and she smiled, holding up her drink like a toast. It was the same damn drink, too.

I held up my hands in a gesture that made it clear what I thought of her.

"Are you ready for the battle, Tira Misu?" The cry came down, and a cheer exploded from all around. I could see a few participants against the railings, but I figured that most of the screams came from video feeds. That proved terrifying, since it sounded like a rather big audience. Which meant a lot of money. Which probably meant death would be on the table.

This really wasn't as fun as Clay had made it sound.

I looked down to the spot where the last fighter had died. There was no sign of her blood, no trace that she'd ever existed, or that she'd expired here.

The cheering died down. I didn't bother answering the question. They wanted a show? Well screw them. All that they'd have would be me hurting somebody else. My stomach turned. I didn't exactly want to do that either. I didn't mind beating on people, but only if they were bad. That four-armed, really tall fighter hadn't been bad. She'd just been doing what she was meant to do, and that had cost her her life.

A door opened at the other end of the arena, maybe thirty feet away.

The figure stepped from the light into the darkness, backlit, and I felt my extremities grow cold. I would recognize that shape anywhere. That form, that walk… even before he meandered into the light where I could see him, I knew who it was.

I swallowed damn hard.

A dark red band of light appeared around the arena, and three words sprung up.

To the death. The light highlighted the figure.

I looked up and Clay looked back at me. The white neon of the word "death" flashed in his eyes. He gave me one of his crooked grins.

"Well, this is a hell of a pickle we've gotten ourselves into now, isn't it?"

"The fighters will get ready for their trial," the voice boomed.

More cheering - so much that it felt like the entire arena was bulging with spectators.

"I don't have a weapon," I said.

Clay was armed to the teeth.

"Here," he grabbed one of his smaller blades, one that I could easily wield, and handed it to me. The crowd cheered more wildly. I took the blade. He grabbed my hand as I did so and looked me deep in the eye, desperate to hold my attention.

"Listen," he said, "they expect a fight to the death, but we don't have to do it."

"If we don't, they'll kill us," I said.

"Not necessarily," he shrugged, but I wasn't convinced.

"You want to be part of the fighter's league?" I offered. "Hurt me. Wound me. It's okay. I'll heal!" I thought of Ian and hoped that he could heal me. "Don't worry about that. Just do what you have to do to become part of this league. This is important to you!"

"Not without you," he said. "Listen, don't worry. I've got this."

He winked at me, and then he stepped back. I tested the blade, felt its weight and balance. The quality of the lighting changed and became bluer. I looked down at my skin, the purple accented by the blue. Clay's eyes looked electric in this light.

He took a step to the left and I matched it. Were we really going to do this?

I remembered seeing that fighter on the ground. Nobody had mourned her, except maybe me. But maybe she'd had a best friend, too. Someone somewhere who missed her tonight.

A giant gong resonated throughout the entire arena.

"Gotta move," Clay said, and he made a step towards me and then faked to the right. I knew what he was doing. I grinned, and I side-stepped with him, blocking his blow. He broke again. The crowd booed as though they'd seen the faked attempt.

We'd always thought we'd been so smart in fighting classes, getting away with these moves. This was a professional audience, and they wanted blood.

My mind reeled towards what I could do. I side-stepped and slipped on mud. I landed on my knees and quickly rolled away before Clay's sword came down. He didn't mean the blow, though, and I knew that he didn't. I stood back up, sword before me to defend myself.

The crowd booed again. The light changed to gold.

DEATH the crimson word flashed around us.

I could see panic settling into his eyes. We had no way out of this. We could throw down our weapons and probably both forfeit our lives, or Clay could walk away. There was no way I could beat Clay. I had strength, but not like him. But I could vanish, and this arena was currently filled with shadows from the viewing gallery above and from the fake hills and flashing lights.

I drew the shadows towards me, folded them over me, even as I stood up and moved. If I could vanish for a little bit, maybe I could buy us some time. If I could draw the shadows around Clay, then he too could vanish, and we could find safety somewhere else. Maybe we could sneak out and nobody would see us. Would that even be possible? They'd found me before.

But I had to try.

Clay's eyes widened and then narrowed a bit as a grin tugged at his lips. He was glad that I was vanishing.

I slipped towards the right and waited. Clay made a show of looking for me. He could probably find me if he really wanted to. He knew the few signs that I left behind.

But he didn't, of course.

I realized that I hadn't been sure if he would or not. My stomach turned, watching Clay put on a show, turning further left, away from me.

The crowd grew quiet, discontented. The light turned blue, the entire arena cast as though underwater.

Which fit the mood. This definitely felt like drowning.

I stared at the boss. She didn't seem annoyed. She seemed amused. Her right hand, each finger bejeweled with a ring, gave a simple quick flick of the wrist, and the old woman from earlier headed to the edge of the arena.

She'd appeared out of nowhere and, unless I was mistaken, she used some of the same shadow-bending abilities I had. She'd vanished and reappeared in them. Well, that settled that. Traded definitely aged at different speeds.

Clay looked up at her, confused, and she smiled. From a distance, it looked like her teeth might not be all straight and human-looking.

"Coookieee?" she said in a simple, elongated question, each syllable like a cold, hard, hit directly on my spine. I felt the power behind the simple word, and

I saw it crumple into Clay, who she'd directed the question at.

His shoulders drooped. His neck bent and his head dropped forward against his chest. He still breathed, but all tension left his body.

I took a step towards him, the blue light making me feel heavy. Clay's limbs flew up as though electrified. His head jerked up and his eyes snapped open. They definitely were electric blue. His usually relaxed stance and his jokey smile were gone, leaving behind only hard edges.

I took a step back, terrified. He homed in on me. His hand reached for a small single-handed crossbow hooked to his hip. He pulled it out and fired. I had no doubt that the shot was meant to kill.

I moved just quickly enough, the bolt cutting across my shoulder. I lost hold of the shadows and threw myself back. All that I had was the sword. I grabbed it as he came ramming toward me, screaming.

The crowd, which had been eerily quiet, erupted into bone-shattering cheers.

"Clay!" I pleaded over the screams, but he came down hard and fast, and I could barely keep his blows at bay, trying to use my greater speed against his strength. But it wasn't enough. It wasn't enough, and all that I could see were the eyes of that dead gladiator from earlier, and how she hadn't seen death coming.

But it had come at the hands of Clay, with the same

sword that he would now cleave me with, possessed by a fury that I couldn't understand or stop.

Terrified, I managed to kick out and catch his feet. He fell to his knees. I took two steps back, not daring to turn, to run from him. Unable to gauge the terrain, I slipped on some mud and landed hard, scrambling to get back up.

He was on me in an instant. I kicked up, pushed him away, used his own speed against him, and sent him flying to the side.

I'd lost my sword. I didn't have a weapon anymore, and Clay stood up so quickly that I didn't even have the time to form a plan. I pushed myself back to my feet, held my hands out defensively, ready to come to blows against the sharp weapon, knowing I would lose.

But Clay's legs suddenly buckled, like something had hurt him.

He fell to one knee, as though in slow motion, clutching his right calf. Something left his side and slithered away through the sand and the grass.

"Tira?" Clay said, as he blinked away the fog of anger and bloodlust.

"Clay," I replied, relieved that he was back. I smiled as I took a step towards him. Before I could reach him, he slumped forward quietly.

I heard his body strike the sand, the arena had grown so hushed. I rushed to his side, not worried about a trap, not even caring anymore. I turned him over on his back. His eyes looked at me—not in the way that they usually looked at me, with a smile, ready to tell a joke, or speak of an adventure, or to be sullen. Nor did they look at me with anger. They looked at me the way that the gladiator's had earlier - vacant, and not quite believing that it had come to this.

I gasped as the crowd caught on and began cheering, as the lights shot various colors of victory across the entire arena. As the voice boomed across the mic system, announcing me as the winner.

I ignored all of those things, my mind blank, unable to process any thought, save one.

Clay was dead.

Clay was dead, and I was alone.

I DIDN'T REMEMBER COMING BACK to the cell. All I remembered was holding Clay. I think I screamed. I tried to bring him back. I'm pretty sure I punched his chest, which I suspect is not how you do CPR, but desperate times...

People grabbed me. I remembered letting go of his head as they pulled my arms back. I remembered it falling on the ground, his neck shifting slightly, as though his dead eyes tried to follow me, his skin turning a bluish color under the lights of the arena.

I wanted to destroy every one of those lights, fold into the shadows, and lose myself in them forever.

But I didn't. I didn't, because it didn't matter anymore. Nothing mattered anymore, save those vacant eyes, looking at me, watching me get dragged away.

I don't really remember after that. I don't know if they knocked me out, but I don't think so. I think I just didn't really want to be here anymore, so I drifted away.

Now I sat in my cell again, alone. My shoulder stung where the bolt had nicked it, but I didn't care about the blood. I was dirty from the mud where I'd fallen, and where I'd been on my knees to collect Clay's body and hold it against me.

None of it mattered. None of the stains or the blood mattered. None of the struggles or the dreams mattered.

Clay was gone.

Clay was gone, and I didn't even know how. Or what had happened. I was angry at the boss, the league, the guild, the entire Traded system, but my anger still lacked direction. It couldn't focus it on one target and so it couldn't ignite, unable to burn away the grief that consumed my soul.

A noise at the door. Someone unlocked it. I remained seated, but felt every single one of my muscles tense up, ready to spring into attack. A wall of fatigue seemed to hold me back, though, so I just stared as the door opened. I was surprised to see Ian step in.

He closed the door quickly.

"Clay's dead," I said before he could say anything.

"We need to go, Tira," he knelt beside me. "We need to go now, while they're not watching."

"Clay's dead," I repeated. Surely he hadn't heard me.

"Come on," he said, not unkindly, pulling me up to my feet.

"Why are you bothering with me," I said. "Clay's dead. I'm not worth it."

"Come on," he said, pulling me to the door. We stepped outside. One of the guards was down, his skin turning purplish-blue, just like Clay's had.

"What got him?" I asked, stunned and confused, my mind slowly wrapping around the possibilities of what had hurt the guard. The same thing that had gotten Clay. That much was certain.

"We have to move quickly," Ian said. He took my arm and gently nudged me down the corridor.

"No," I held my ground. "Ian, what got him? It's the same thing that got Clay."

"Do you trust me?" Ian asked.

I looked into his dark eyes. That was a loaded question. Did I trust anyone right now? I didn't know. I didn't even know if I trusted myself.

"Did you do this?" I asked, pointing towards the guard.

"We can still save Clay," Ian offered, his voice soft, as though afraid he would break me, "but we have to move quickly."

"He's not dead?" I said, unbelieving..

"He doesn't need to *stay* dead," Ian said. "We have to go quickly. Come on. Please!" he added for good measure, his desperation beginning to ring in his words.

I nodded and followed him down the corridor, the sight of the guard haunting me. Ian had done this. Ian had stopped Clay. Ian had saved my life. Ian had killed Clay.

By the time this day was over, there was a very real possibility that I would stab Ian to death.

31

AFTER FOLLOWING Ian-the-dog for so long, it was distracting to have a human walking in front of me. He seemed equally uncomfortable with his two legs, and downright annoyed by stairs.

He clutched the handrail way more tightly than necessary. He must spend most of his time as a dog, or another animal. I can't say I really blamed him for that. Being human, or human-like, I suppose, just downright sucked at times.

We went down six flights of stairs and reached the basement. I wrapped the shadows around us. Someone might be able to break them down, sure, but maybe not. It was worth the risk, though the shadows didn't offer their usual comfort.

Once we'd reached the basement, Ian hesitated. He pushed on the door and looked in quickly. I put my hand on his arm, indicating that I would go first, and that he should stay close to me.

I didn't have a weapon on me again, of course. What was it with me and weapons? I loved weapons, but I couldn't keep hold of them at all. I'd have to get better at concealing them. I glanced at Ian, wondering if he had any weapons hidden on him. Not that he needed to. He seemed to be his own best weapon.

The corridor past the door was clear, and the lighting was dim—typical creepy basement stuff. I loved it. I wrapped the shadows around me and Ian more tightly and stepped in quietly, held the door for Ian to follow, and let it slide silently closed.

The basement smelled as humid as the cell upstairs had, except in a more comforting way, like it was *supposed* to smell dank here. Ian indicated that we should move forward down the corridor, and so I did, quietly. I could smell something else mixed in with the humidity. Something not quite as pleasant.

Death. Death was definitely in the air.

This was why we were here. The body disposal area. I swallowed hard, a lump in my raw throat.

I hoped Ian hadn't lied to me. My ankle moved with just a little bit of discomfort, reminding me of what Ian had managed to do already. Maybe this was why he wasn't changing back into an animal - so that he could preserve his strength to heal Clay.

I crossed an open door and glanced in, practically

giddy to spot a janitor's closet. I shot Ian a grin and slipped in. The contents were disappointingly sparse. Cleanliness mustn't have ranked high on their list of concerns.

I grabbed a mop handle and a rusty metal dustpan, all dinged up from overuse and with layers of dust on it. Oh, this would be perfect. I couldn't wait to get in a fight, now.

Ian's eyebrows were in his "really?" position when I rejoined him, making sure the shadows were wrapped around us. I offered him the dustpan, but he shook his head. His eyebrows didn't move as he did so.

His loss.

We moved down the barely illuminated hallway, until he held up two fingers, pointed to an opened door, and then down the corridor.

Two doors down. I nodded, loosened my grip on the mop handle to move quickly with it if needed.

What was in the first door, I wondered? Maybe somebody waiting to get a broom handle in their eye? Or a dustpan across the throat? Hitting some*thing*, preferably some*one*, would make me feel a hell of a lot better.

I glanced in. It was disappointingly empty, except for old trash compactors.

Some of the death smell definitely came from here. This was an older building, with trash chutes from various floors leading down, and it stank like about a hundred years' worth of garbage. Some refuse tumbled down as we watched, and crashed into one of the bins.

Gross.

We reached the second door, this one closed. I nudged it open, pleased that it didn't screech open. Not that it mattered. No one was here either. A blast of cold air was all that greeted us.

I stepped in, closed the door behind Ian. A single bulb lit the space, and I gasped at the sight. We stood inside a giant cold room, holding the bodies of recent dead. The multi-armed woman was here, her tall body only partially on a slab. There was no ceremony, no blanket covering her.

I felt even more terrible for her.

And on another slab lay Clay. His eyes were closed, and he was still very blue. My breath caught in my throat.

Ian quietly crossed the floor to reach him.

"Give me a moment," he said. I followed him, looked at Clay. I always felt that dead bodies should look more peaceful than they actually did. Like they should reflect that moment where you stepped into the afterlife and discovered peace.

But that hadn't been my experience with bodies, and Clay was no different.

"Are you going to heal him?" I asked Ian, my voice catching in my throat.

"No," he said. "I have something else for this."

He reached in his pocket and pulled out a syringe. It was already filled with liquid. I narrowed my eyes, watched him as he pushed it deep into Clay's chest.

"This might startle him," he said, and he injected the liquid in.

Clay's limbs shot up, his eyes wide, and a shudder travelled through his whole body as he gasped for air. His skin tone immediately became warmer, the blue only clinging to his lips and to his extremities.

"Clay!" I choked on his name. He was still lying down and looked confused. "Are you alright?" I asked. He nodded and tried to stand up.

"Don't move too quickly," Ian said. "You're going to feel this."

"What happened?" he asked, hoarse. I couldn't answer him. I couldn't believe I was actually talking to him—that he was still alive.

"We should go," Ian said, looking at me, a plea in his eyes. "Before they figure out you're gone and come looking for you."

"That's a good idea. Can you stand, Clay?"

He nodded, but we still helped him, Ian on one side and me on the other. We headed towards the exit at the back, a few heartbeats away from (temporary) freedom.

3 2

———

THERE WEREN'T **many places** where Traded could recover, unless they went to a guild. We couldn't exactly go to a guild right now, considering that the Guild of Shadows expected us to show up with the canister, and the fighter's league would come looking for us, or at least me. Not Clay, since they thought he was dead. Or Ian, since they thought he was a dog.

Of course, if they ditched me, the two of them could just stroll into a coffee shop and enjoy a cappuccino. They could pass as human and I couldn't, and I was the one being hunted. This whole thing was getting ridiculous. Night wrapped around us as we headed to the one place we could go: the halfway house.

"This is stupid," I said. "I mean, won't they look for us here right away?" The place still seemed deserted. Ian shrugged.

"I don't know. I mean, this place is pretty much shut down. They might think that you'd just run out of town and leave, which most smart people would do…"

Clay shot me a grin. I returned it. It felt so good to see him do that again.

"Maybe we should just do that," Clay said. "Just run out of town. Leave."

"They'd find us," I said. I looked to Ian for confirmation.

"They would," he confirmed. "I'm sorry."

"It's hardly your fault," I said. "So, what's our next step, then? I mean, we have to join a guild, don't we?"

"We do," Clay said. He leaned back against the wall on his bed. I sat at the end of the same bed. Ian stood near us. He still didn't seem very comfortable. Maybe staying in human form this long grated on him. I wondered if he could shift now, and chose not to, to better guide us.

"Can we just go join another guild?" I asked nobody in particular. "I mean, really, the main point is that we get to hang out, right? So what if we go to another guild? Something different."

Clay didn't answer, but I could tell by his silence that he really just wanted to go back to the fighter's league, even though he'd given his life to them once already.

"Once you're marked," Ian said, "you're meant for a guild. You can't just change your mind."

"That hardly seems fair," I said. "We were told that they were invitations, not orders."

"Well, you were told wrong," Ian said, not unkindly. "The fighter's league will want Clay back. The second they find out he's still alive, they'll come for him."

"Nobody wants me," I said.

"You can come to the fighter's league with me," Clay insisted. "I'm sure they were impressed with what you did back there. I mean, you won against me. And I'm not easy to beat." He gave me a grin. "But also, you managed to escape, and you brought me back to life! You'll be a hero after this!"

"Why do you even want to go back there? I mean, they killed you!"

"Yeah, kind of. If I'm fast enough, though, and smart enough, I should be able to live. I can also not do death fights," he shrugged. "I might have been a tad over-enthused there."

"You signed up for death fights? On purpose?" I asked, eyes wide.

He sighed. "It's the most glory, you know?" He continued before I could wrap my mind around his stupidity. "And it's not that bad a place. Even without the bigger fights, I still get to battle, I can get some glory if I win, and I think I'd do well. Well, not against you," he shrugged. "But I don't want to hurt you."

"But you'll make friends there," I said, "and you'll have to fight those friends!"

"I don't make friends that easily." A dark mood descended on him quickly.

"Well. I don't know. You and Blake could be BFFs."

He snorted.

"Seriously, though," Clay said, "you should consider it. Come with me. Be a part of something different! Hang out together still."

"Sure, until you get killed," I said bitterly. "Which I don't think will take that long, at this rate. I mean, that old woman made you go berserk, or something. You went insane!"

"Yeah, that was weird." He looked perplexed. "It's like I lost control and I just wanted to hurt everything around me."

"Great," I muttered.

"I'm sure that that won't happen again."

Nice that one of us thought so.

He pushed on. "Well, if we have to go somewhere, it might as well be somewhere that I'm going to enjoy before I go," he spoke softly, with none of his usual brashness. It made his words more powerful. "We're Traded, Tira. How long can we really believe we're going to survive in this world anyways?"

I sighed. I didn't really have a counter-argument. Everyone and everything seemed pretty intent on killing us right now.

"I don't really have anywhere else to go. I might as well stay with you, Clay. But no death fights. Seriously.

Let's at least try to survive a bit longer. If you die, I'll just join a circus guild and curse you forever."

"Blake would never let you live it down," Clay said with a large grin.

"Oh, I know. I'd have to beat him into letting it go."

Clay laughed as we fell back into our old patterns. I noticed that Ian stood very quietly beside us. I shifted to look at him.

"What about you, Ian?" I said. "Can you change guilds? Do you want to join the league with us?" Clay stiffened at the suggestion.

"I should go," Ian said. Before I could protest, he'd stepped outside of the room, reaching the exit quickly.

"I'll be back," I said.

"Want me to follow?" Clay asked.

"Nah. Get some sleep. I'll be right back." And I slipped out after Ian into the shadows, hoping that he wouldn't vanish into a mouse before I got to ask him what the hell was wrong with him.

Ian moved pretty fast, but I was faster, more used to two-legged running than he was. He stuck to a quiet street, thank goodness, lined with old wooden fences.

"Where are you going?" I said. He stopped, looking annoyed. Maybe even angry. I didn't let that stop me, coming up to him.

He sighed.

"Can't you just let it go?" he said. "Why do you have to make everything so complicated?"

"*I'm* making everything so complicated?" I protested. "I'm just trying to find out where you're going and why you're being all sulky. I mean, just leaving like this is a *great* idea! It's not like there are people trying to kill us or anything."

"They're not going to try to kill me," he said. He seemed to regret his words immediately. He took a deep breath. "Look, you're in danger. You have to be careful and you have to be smart."

"Okay," I said. "Care to tell me what you seem to know that I don't?"

"Look, Tira, you can't just…" He looked even more frustrated, like he searched for words that evaded him. He sighed, the fight drained out of him. "Everyone gets summoned to a guild, Tira. It's the way of the Traded."

"I wasn't," I said. "But it's okay. Maybe I was summoned by the fighter's league, and I just didn't know until now. Maybe I'm part and parcel with Clay. I mean, if you say they've been watching us this entire time, then they must have known that that's the way to get us in, right? You get one, you get the other. We're better together, anyways. We always have been."

Ian observed me for a few moments. I had a feeling that he wasn't about to support my argument.

"You received a hair barrette," Ian said, his voice so soft that I barely heard him. "You received a barrette on your last day of school."

I blinked a couple of times, absorbing the information. I had. I'd completely forgotten about it until now. I pulled it out, the dark item reflecting no light in my hand. I observed it more closely, something I hadn't bothered doing. The infinity symbol seemed to fold in two, if I bent the barrette.

I glanced up at Ian, then folded the barrette. It

followed my movement, a small needle appearing from below the symbol.

"That wouldn't have killed you," Ian quickly said. "It's just a sleeping agent, which could prove useful to you."

"If I knew it was there and didn't prick myself, anyway," I mumbled, folding the barrette back, satisfied with the slight click.

"This doesn't look like an invitation," I said. "It looks like a weapon."

"The best things serve double duty, Tira," Ian said, then looked up at me. "It's the way of the Guild of Shadows."

The Guild of Shadows. I remembered Sonsil's words. *We keep the balance.*

"Why not tell me?" I whispered.

Ian finally looked me in the eye when he answered.

"It's a very different guild, and very selective," he said. "We need to make sure we have the right people, even those selected."

"You brought me there," I said, working through all of the details and possibilities. There were so few of them. "You're one of them, and you stayed with me…" I whispered.

He nodded. This time when he spoke, he didn't look me in the eye.

"I was sent to assess you after you left school. Keep an eye on you, hide in my animal shapes as necessary.

Make sure that you survived long enough to be of use to the Guild of Shadows and see where your loyalties lay. With Clay, or with the Guild."

"I don't know the Guild," I said.

"I know," Ian said, his voice matching the softness of mine. "But *we* know *you*."

Well I hated the sound of that. I narrowed my eyes at him.

"How did you do that to Clay?" The question seemed to surprise Ian. He looked me in the eye again.

"I know how to use poisons," he said. "It's part of what the Guild of Shadows can do. Something a little bit more quiet, a little bit less detectable. I used one on him, and just had to reach him in time to revive him without any danger."

"Oh," I said. "Well, that's good."

He nodded, waited for me to continue.

"That's how we found Clay so easily when the guild had him, isn't it? You've just been pulling me along this entire time."

"No, not fully," Ian said, "but somewhat, I'll admit. A lot of that you managed by yourself. A lot of the things that happened, well, I couldn't have predicted."

"You were sent to protect me," I said. He shook his head.

"No. But I owed you one. When you got me out of that room. I had been trapped in dog form, and I couldn't change back. One of the most annoying features of my powers. You got me out before I got killed. That's not a bad thing."

"Who'd have killed you?"

"I don't know," he shrugged. "I really don't know who those people were, or why they collected what they did. But the Guild of Shadows wants them now, starting with that canister. And so we'll have to go and get them."

"All those dead animals…"

"I know," he said, his voice stricken by grief. "They killed them, collecting something from them. All those different pieces, they boiled down and stuck in that canister. We're not sure why, but Sonsil is worried about it. I've rarely seen Sonsil worried about anything."

"He likes animals?" I asked.

"He doesn't like innocents getting killed," he sighed again. "Like the little girl you saved from the fire."

"During Clay's test?" This wasn't getting any less puzzling.

"That wasn't a test for him."

"Oh." In retrospect, that made some sense. Why would a fighter's league test someone without having them fight? I narrowed my eyes at him. "Would the Guild have saved the little girl, if I hadn't?"

He nodded. "The little girl is one of our operatives. She could have saved herself."

"She gave me up!" I spat out.

He shrugged. "We needed to see what you'd do then, too. You could have run, or denied it."

"You were testing my moral fiber?" My eyebrows must have been near my hairline now.

"Like I said, we keep the balance. There are tough choices to be made, Tira."

My head hurt. I wanted to go back and check on Clay, make sure he was safe.

"Okay," I said. "So, what happens now?"

"The Guild of Shadows still needs you to get that canister back from the fighter's league," he paused and lowered his voice. "We're not sure on the league's involvement in this, and why they had Clay collect it. We know that they've wanted Clay for a long time, though, and he's been marked as theirs," he looked down, his voice softening further. "And I can't help you anymore, so you'll have to decide whether or not you can trust Clay to have your back."

"I can trust Clay!" I protested and then immediately questioned my words. Ian wasn't wrong. Clay was so focused on his goal of joining the fighter's league that I may be a casualty in his ambition's wake.

No, not Clay. Clay had died. Clay would have preferred to die than destroy me. I had to trust my friend.

"You can retrieve the canister with Clay's help, or on your own. But certainly not with my help. I'm sorry, Tira, but this is as far as I can go. My instructions are clear, and I am bound to the Guild of Shadows. As are you," he added. "Remember that. You can't just join the fighter's league. The Guild of Shadows will come for you."

"I have no doubt of that," I whispered. "So, I guess this is goodbye?"

"For now," he said. He looked like he wanted to say something more or maybe change into something else and skirt away into the darkness. But he did neither of those things, simply turning and walking away down the street. I watched him go until he was out of sight.

I headed back to the halfway house, and to Clay. We had some planning to do if we were going to succeed and get out with our lives intact.

As I walked, I analyzed the few days we'd been out of school, with a lens of being manipulated by the Guild of Shadows instead of the fighters' league, like I'd originally thought.

And I didn't like what I spotted.

Stealing the canister. Clay choosing to leave me behind to bring it to the fighter's league. Me going after Clay. Now having to choose between Clay and the Guild.

I could see that they'd manipulated the situation, sure. But I also saw that Clay had willingly followed a certain path.

And I didn't think he would swerve from it now, no

matter how well he meant, or how much he cared for our friendship.

I hated that the Guild of Shadows had cast such a harsh light on our friendship. I feared it might disintegrate in its wake.

3 4

I FOUND Clay on the bed, wide awake. He'd obviously been waiting, and I wouldn't be surprised if he'd crawled in just before me, having followed me out to make sure I was safe.

"Hey," I said, and sat down on the edge of the bed.

"Hey," he answered. "You good?"

"Yeah. I imagine you overheard?"

"Sorry."

"No, it's okay. I'd have done the same thing."

"I'm just not used to us having secrets, you know?" he said.

"But you've been keeping so many," I whispered. "You didn't tell me about the fighter's league, or about the canister, or any of it. Clay, this is serious, we're not in school anymore. We're going to get ourselves killed!"

He looked embarrassed. "You're right, I've been thinking a lot about that. You know, now that I've come back to life and all that, and I'm sorry. Look, I don't exactly know what's going on either. But I remember hearing all of the stories about the fighter's leagues and all of the gladiators and heroes of the ring, and I just know that's where I want to be, you know?" His eyes shone with youthful enthusiasm. "I just want to get a chance to make a mark. Have some fun. Meet some people. But, I want to do all those things with you."

I loved that he wanted to stay with me. I loved that we'd made it work for thirteen years. I even loved that, no matter what he'd overheard, of being manipulated by the Guild of Shadows, his main concern was getting to join his favorite league.

"I don't know if that's possible," I told Clay. "You heard what Ian said. I got an invitation from the Guild of Shadows. I just didn't realize it." I pulled out the barrette, dark metal with an infinity sign. It reflected no light.

"Yeah, not noticing something so obvious sounds like you," he said sarcastically. I playfully punched his shoulder. He sobered up, looked at me seriously.

"You just don't notice what's right in front of you sometimes, Tira."

"I don't notice? *You* don't notice either!"

He paused.

"Oh yeah? What's right in front of me right now?" he whispered.

I hesitated for a brief second. "I am."

He looked at me for a few moments, the silence stretching into eternity as I waited for him to say something more.

"You are," Clay finally said, for which I was grateful, stopping my mind and my heart from spinning at rates that the world couldn't quite match. "And I'd like it to stay this way. Can we still be friends if we're in different guilds?" he asked, his voice cracking a bit.

"I think so," I said, "but I don't know. I just…I don't know a whole lot of anything right now."

"I know we have to get that canister back tomorrow," Clay said, "*together*. And I know we'll do better if we sleep."

"You're right about that," I hesitated for a few seconds and then moved into the bed beside him, took off my boots, and removed as much of my clothes as I could while remaining decent. I snuggled under the rough sheets. The mattress was firm and not that comfortable, but certainly more comfortable than sleeping against a wall.

And Clay wasn't dead. That made a hell of a difference too.

"I'm glad you're here," I told Clay.

"I'm glad you're here," he whispered. He looked like wanted to say something else, but before he could, my eyelids grew heavy, and I was fast asleep, still clutching the barrette in my hands, Ian and Clay's words chasing me into restless dreams.

THE BUILDING which held the fighter's league seemed more threatening in daylight. My hood covered my face, my hands stuck deep in my pockets, my heart thudding in my ears. Clay practically vibrated beside me, more so as we climbed the concrete steps leading to the door.

I didn't fold the shadows around me. It was pointless, and this was a show of good faith.

Clay cast a grin my way before he pushed the door open. I tried to freeze that grin in my mind. Clay *always* shot grins my way. But there were different types of grins. Happy ones, and sad ones. This was a definite mix.

I followed Clay up the stairs to the weird office space. The tall blonde woman looked ecstatic to see him. I stayed back, not folding the shadows on me, but definitely staying near them, my hood still up.

"How are you alive?" the pale man asked, clasping hands with Clay. "I told you you shouldn't have registered for death fights so early on!"

Clay looked embarrassed. "Ya, I shoulda listened," he said, then glanced my way. "This is my friend, Tira. She saved me." That wasn't completely true, but I stepped out into the light and pulled down my hood.

I held my breath, but nobody screamed. I guess they'd already seen me, but I still expected a negative reaction. The blonde woman crossed the floor.

"Do you hug?" she asked.

"I, um, I guess?" She gathered me in her arms and hugged me fiercely, like I was her best friend. It was nice, if a bit uncomfortable. I was just glad she wasn't running away screaming.

She broke her embrace, her hands still on my shoulders. "Thank you. We like Clay."

"I like him, too," I agreed, and she gave me a knowing smile. I blushed. Clay chatted with the two men at the back. She glanced back at me. "He really wants you to join," she said. "He's been talking about it for years."

"You've known him for years," I didn't ask so much as stated, wrapping my heart around the secrets my best friend had been keeping from me. All those heists, his "contacts," his enthusiasm for battles. It had all been to feed his entry into this league.

No wonder he seemed so at home here. More than that. He seemed happy in a way I'd rarely seen.

"He'll be okay here," I said, not meaning to voice the words. But the woman nodded.

"He will be, sugar," she said kindly. "We'll keep an eye out for him."

"No more death fights?" I held her eyes, to see if I could spot a lie there. But I couldn't, the gold flecks at their center unguarded.

"No more death fights," she said. "At least, not for a while yet."

"Fair enough," I whispered, and broke away from the woman to join Clay. He'd already been tested for years. They knew he belonged, that he had the grit to succeed and was a good fit.

As I watched him wave goodbye to the three frontline workers, or guards, probably, my heart felt free for him, and heavier for myself.

He was with his people.

We crossed the cubicles, the carpet and walls still as ugly. People were truly happy to see him. A few thanked me for saving him, and they seemed genuine. The old woman stepped out of her office and nodded at me. I nodded back, not sure what we'd shared. But she stepped back and closed her door, as though she didn't intend to mingle.

Or interfere.

As she turned, a dark shape caught my eye - a barrette holding up her hair in a proper updo. It didn't reflect the light, though she was too far from me to see if it bore an infinity symbol.

The Guild of Shadows. Maintaining the balance. Infiltrating leagues and Traded organizations, to ensure everything continued in safety. Like Clay's league. And Clay's obvious dreams. Before we reached the boss' door, he took my hand and pulled me to the side, into an empty office.

He closed the door. No one followed or questioned him. They trusted him. They cared for him and respected him. My heart ached, but I couldn't quite tell why anymore.

"Look, I've been looking into this Guild of Shadows," Clay said, looking concerned and uncomfortable.

"Oh?" I said, feeling numb, "and what did you find out?"

"They sound real bad, Tira," he closed the gap between us. "Look, I know the fighter's league ain't all that great, I mean, a lot of people die here, and it's all for gambling and sport. But the Guild of Shadows? Nobody really knows much, except to fear them. They kill people. It's not entertainment-based, it's some real screwed-up stuff they do. I think you should stay here. Stay with the fighter's league. Stay with me."

"You know I can't," I whispered. "I have to go to the Guild of Shadows. That's my guild. Look, I'll make this work!" I added when he looked so stricken. "I swear, I won't kill anyone unless they deserve it."

"You won't have a choice," he said. "I mean, I know that their whole goal is to kill people who've stepped out of line or are too dangerous, but the stories are that they pretty much kill anyone who gets in their way."

"Well, I'll be the exception," I said. "I have my own code. You know that. I can make it work."

"You think they'll leave you that choice?" he said.

"I'll make sure they do. Just like you have a choice not to fight in death battles," he looked embarrassed again. "Besides," I added softly, "you found your people here, Clay. It's time for me to try to find mine. I'm a demon, aren't I?" I gave a short laugh. "I might as well go find some other demons in the shadows."

He didn't join me in the laugh like he usually would. His eyes grew more serious, deep, dark pools without a ripple, all of the weight of the world contained within them. He leaned closer.

"You're the least demonic person I know," he whispered, and his lips met mine, sending an electric jolt through my entire body. I allowed myself to become lost in that kiss for a few moments before breaking free. We both struggled to catch our breath.

"We'll still be friends," I whispered. And then I reached up and kissed him gently again.

"Always," he said, the sorrow in his eyes palpable. Before I could hesitate, I broke from him and opened the door.

If I'd learned one thing as a Traded, it was that choice might not be yours, but the expectations certainly were. Neither one of us could afford to fail, even though I wished for nothing more than to stay here, with him, forever.

"How do we do this?" he asked as we stood before the boss' door.

"I have a plan," I grinned his way, the same grin he usually used on me. "You'll just have to trust me." For a second, I saw hesitation in his eyes, and then he nodded.

This time, I would take the lead. I'd make sure he was fine, and that I would be fine, too. I indicated that he should go in. As he walked in, I wrapped the shadows around me and pulled the barrette free from my hair, unclicking the needle.

Ian wouldn't have lied about a sleeping agent. He'd let me know to test me.

Another test.

But one I had to pass. Betraying my oldest friend. Choosing the Guild over Clay. Not that it felt much like a choice, all roads leading to this moment. To think, all this time, I'd been worried about Clay betraying me.

I took a deep breath as Clay greeted the boss, who

had clearly been informed of his survival. She seemed pleased and not at all surprised to see him.

I wondered if the fighter's league had been working with the Guild of Shadows all along.

Probably. More than likely. I hesitated, my anger rising at the thought that we'd been manipulated so effectively. But I didn't fool myself into thinking we weren't being watched and judged at this very moment. And that our lives were on the line.

I reached out and pricked Clay in the upper arm. He felt the slight sting, the poison acting immediately. He turned to where he knew I hid, hurt in his eyes.

It cut my soul, but I backed away as he toppled down, holding the shadows around me as the boss and her goons headed toward the fallen fighter. I felt better, seeing that they cared. Well, most of them cared. The boss looked around with suspicion. I slipped behind them all, sight unseen, grabbing the canister from behind her desk.

I glanced Clay's way one more time, just in case I never saw him again, and swallowed hard.

Stay safe, a silent wish.

Then I stepped out, folded deep in the shadows, finally accepting that this darkness would be the only place where I truly belonged.

Sonsil regarded the canister, looking pleased. I stood in front of him, not feeling all that pleased. I mean, I'd accomplished what I'd set out to do. Clay was safe, and would be happy in the fighter's league.

But I'd betrayed him. He'd expected us to talk our way through it, or fight. Those were his two modes of operation. Not me. I stuck to the shadows. It's what I was good at. This guild obviously knew it.

"Well done," Sonsil said. "the Guild is pleased with how you handled the mission."

"This entire thing was a pain," I said. He looked surprised, but didn't stop me. "I expect a bit more information next time, and better weapons. Maybe ones that can't be so easily taken from me."

He nodded, as though those were the simplest

requests in the world. "I think you'll fit in here, Ms. Misu."

"I hope so," I said. I wanted to ask if I would see Clay again, but held my peace. I vowed that I would. I'd find a way to him, regularly, and we would still have fun together. Most of this life was out of my control, sure, but I could still have fun wading through it.

I'd make sure of it.

Ian stepped into the room, nodded at me, looking displeased. I wondered if he'd changed into an animal since yesterday. From his grumpy demeanor, I imagined he hadn't.

"You've met my second, I understand?"

The second of the Guild of Shadows. That's what Ian was. Had been all along. And here I thought he'd basically lived in the bush and was an unwilling operative.

I was such a fool. I really had to learn how to pick my friends better. As did Clay, apparently.

"You trust that she'll be good for the guild?" The leader asked Ian. Ian looked me in the eye, but then glanced away again.

"I do," he said without hesitation.

"Then welcome to the Guild of Shadows, Ms. Misu. There will be a lot of work here, but I think you'll find it quite rewarding."

And just like that, I was dismissed. I stepped outside,

where someone waited for me, not to throw me in jail or beat me, but to show me to the room where I'd be staying with other new trainees of the Guild.

I was home. They wanted me here. They'd chosen me. And they'd done a piss poor job of validating the entire experience.

But still, this was home, now. As much as it could be without Clay.

I vowed to find a way to make this work. I would find a way to belong, and to do what needed to be done. And to keep my word to Clay. To always remain true to myself. I had to make sure of that. Come hell or high water.

I grinned. I'd definitely make this work. But I'd have to find a way to make it work *my way.*

After all, there was no point in being a demon unless you raised a little hell.

-The End-

THE GUILD OF SHADOWS 2:
HELL BENT

There's something in the shadows... and for once, it's not me.

I'm Tira Misu, wielder of darkness and initiate of the Guild of Shadows. I fight like a demon (okay, I look like one, too), but I'm no monster. At least, not this time.

But make no mistake, there is a monster out there, and right now, it's taking down the Traded, one unfortunate body at a time.

The problem? I'm the only one who can find it.

The solution? Make damned sure I have fun doing so.

ABOUT THE AUTHOR

Marie Bilodeau is an Ottawa-based author and storyteller, with eight published books to her name. Her speculative fiction has won several awards and has been translated into French (Les Éditions Alire) and Chinese (SF World). Her short stories have also appeared in various anthologies. In a past life not-so-long ago, she was Deputy Publisher for The Ed Greenwood Group (TEGG). Marie is also a storyteller and has told stories across Canada in theatres, tea shops, at festivals and under disco balls. She's won story slams with personal stories, has participated in epic tellings at the National Arts Centre, and has adapted classical material.

Marie is co-host of the Archivos Podcast Network with Dave Robison, co-chair of Ottawa's speculative fiction literary convention CAN-CON with Derek Künsken, and is a casual blogger at Black Gate Magazine.

Find out more and see pretty book covers at www.mariebilodeau.com.